The giggle, a grating, hateful sou[nd] didn't dare look for its source.

"This Emperor's Delight is dank," Trey said sitting across from her in the Chinese restaurant. "I can't wait to dig in." He took his fork and stabbed the fish which flopped its tail on the plate. With his knife, he cut off a piece of flesh and blood spurted all over the hot metal plate. It steamed and clotted.

"No," Tricia mouthed, horrified by the sight. The nightmare was happening again.

"Oh sorry," Trey said. "Are you one of those old-fashioned snacks who thinks a guy should wait until she takes her first bite?" He stuck another piece of gore into his mouth. "Not this guy. Mm, this is so good." A drop of blood slid from the corner of his mouth and spilled onto his shirt.

"Want to try some?" he said, cutting off a piece and holding the bloody chunk on his fork for her to sample.

"No, thank you," she said. "I—I'm not crazy about fish."

The trout on Trey's plate rolled an opaque eye in its socket to stare at her. It seemed to be smiling.

Faint laughter rippled from the direction of the entryway. She turned toward the sound and saw the malevolent Asian woman leering at her. The evil spirit shimmered and faded like a watercolor painting dropped in a fountain.

Tricia knew she had not seen the last of her.

She looked down at the maggots roiling on her plate and projectile vomited on Trey.

VINCENT COURTNEY

Cover art and design by David Dodd

First Crossroad Press Edition - 2023

A NOTE FROM THE AUTHOR

Greeting, boils and ghouls. To my delight, the good folks at Crossroad Press contacted me about republishing my horror books from the nineties. It isn't often you get a chance to hop into the Wayback Machine to revisit books that were published thirty years ago. After reading them, I still loved the stories but wasn't that happy with some of my writing crap, er, craft. So, I decided to apply three decades of writing experience to fix what needed fixing and update each book while keeping the '90s horror vibe.

I now present *Deadly Diet*.

I hope you're hungry for a heaping spoonful of fear.

PART ONE

ONE

Tricia Hall woke to the sound of whispering in her bedroom. At first, she thought the voices were part of her dream. She had been back at Viera High standing in front of an empty bench near the theater department. Megan and Mandy, her BFFs since grade school should have been sitting there but they were not. Oddly, she could hear them talking to each other about lame classes and guys who didn't know they existed and how junk food was blowing up their current diet plans, you know the usual, but she couldn't see them anywhere. Tricia tried to follow the sound of their voices but could not place from which direction they were coming. She wandered the hallways, uneasy and vaguely frightened. Every time she turned a corner, she expected to see the M&M's giggling at her. Instead, she encountered hostile pale strangers, all dressed in black, staring at her with barely concealed contempt, pointing their pallid fingers at her, accusing Tricia of what she couldn't say. She woke up before one of the girls could touch her with a cold fingertip.

And now...

She heard voices. Coming from inside her bedroom. Devious whispers too low for her to make out what was being said. She kept the side of her face glued to the pillow, eyes wide, listening. The first voice was that of a little girl, strangely muffled, as if she were lying in a lined coffin. The other voice was more disturbing. It was similar to that of the girl, yet possessed of an otherworldly quality, not quite human.

Tricia told herself that she was imagining things. That it was the television in the living room. Dad was always falling asleep on the couch in there and leaving it on. That was what she heard.

But she had seen her father go to bed earlier, tired from a long day at work. And Mom had banned television from their bedroom as watching it at night disrupted her circadian rhythms. So, who was in her bedroom talking?

The conversation stopped cold.

An insinuation of observation crept into Tricia's awareness. She could feel the intruders there in the darkness. Now silent. Watching her. Did they know that she was awake and listening to them? What was it that they didn't want her to hear?

Rustling. A creak of wood. Someone was moving.

She rolled over onto her back in the bed but couldn't bring herself to look anywhere other than the ceiling. What if the outsiders were there at the foot of the bed, knives out? Waiting for her to look down into their rabid faces, relishing her terror before they pounced, stabbing and slashing. She recalled her little sister Penny being afraid to go to bed that night because some of the kids at her new kindergarten had told her that the town of Bitterbrook was haunted. Was that what was in her room with Tricia, spirits stalking her from the shadows?

She stared at the ceiling, her heart pounding, trying to find the guts to sit up and debunk the ghost story that she had created in her mind. She closed her eyes and repeated the mantra: *Nothing is there. Nothing is there.* She took a deep breath and forced herself to sit up and look.

In a dim blue square of moonlight coming from the window over the oak chest, Tricia saw a tiny girl. The smiling child stared at her, but she saw no life in her glassy eyes. The child didn't move at all. Her white teeth appeared sharp enough to cleanly bite off a finger.

Deadly Diet

Tricia pulled the blanket to her chin and closed her eyes. *You're not there. You're not there. You're just my imagination. A trick of light and shadow.* She looked again. The tiny girl with the hungry grin remained, watching her with those lifeless eyes.

Waiting.

But for what? What was she going to do?

And where was the other girl? In her mind, Tricia pictured her, her eyes glittering with moonlight and madness, crawling toward the bed, knife between her teeth. Coming to kill her so the two of them could feast.

A rustle of fabric came from the direction of the tiny girl. Weight shifted on creaking wood. There was a thump.

Tricia opened her eyes.

The tiny dead girl now sat on the floor in a pool of moonlight, staring up at her, smiling her ravenous grin.

Oh God.

The tiny girl—the ghost—rose from the floor, floating in mid-air, savoring her gasp of fear. At any moment, Tricia expected to see the ghost hurtle toward her, shrieking, jaws open obscenely wide.

But the ghost remained suspended above the floor.

Watching her.

Waiting.

Why do you just float there, grinning at me? What are you waiting for?

The chilling answer tightened the skin on her scalp.

The other girl was waiting for her otherworldly companion to pounce.

And then Tricia saw a pair of small hands holding the tiny waist of the doll, a trace of forearms fading into the shadows.

"Damn it, Penny!" Tricia cried.

Her six-year-old sister's sharp cry made her jump.

She reached over and turned on the light. "What the hell are you doing in here?"

"Nothing, fatty patty yam butt," Penny barked, clutching her Suzy Chatterbox doll to her chest, her eyes wide with fright. She was in her sleeping bag atop the big oak chest in the corner of the room.

"I told you to quit calling me that, you little turdpile. And you and your dumb doll are the ones in my room waking me up with your blabbing."

"We was having a nice talk and you scared us. I'm gonna tell Mom that you did it on a purpose and that you said the D word and the H word in front of me." She clambered out of her sleeping bag. The determined look on her face signaled that the powers-that-be were about to receive an unfavorable report about big sister.

"Wait, I didn't mean to scare you. You woke me up and I …" thought there were ghosts in the room, Tricia almost said, but this explanation would scare Penny even more and bolster her case against her. Better to go on offense.

"Why did you sneak into my room without my permission anyway?"

Penny huffed and looked at her doll. "We was in my bed and Suzy got scared of the ghosts and wanted to come in here. Right, Suzy?"

Penny squeezed the index finger of her right hand.

"Yes, Momsuds." The doll answered in Penny's tape-recorded voice, revealing the source of the otherworldly voice Tricia had heard. That dumb doll was her sister's favorite toy. She talked into its ear and a miniature tape recorder would record up to five different messages to play back whenever Penny squeezed the appropriate digit on the doll's right hand.

"Wait, Pen. Were you worried about what those little dopes at school told you about Bitterbrook being haunted? Because that is so BS. A town can't be haunted."

"But that's what they said and they're my new friends, so I have to believe them. They told me ghosts live here."

"Just because they're new friends doesn't mean they won't mess with you. You're a newbie, so they decided to play a trick on you and tell you a scary story. Don't believe any of that stuff about ghosts."

Why not, Tricia? You believed it a minute ago.

"But I don't believe any of that spooky stuff, Tricia Wisha. I told you it's Suzy that does. She's the one who asked me to take her to your room. She said it made her feel safe."

Deadly Diet

When Tricia realized that Penny had been legit terrified about the town being haunted, her anger melted. She pulled back the blanket, inviting her little sister to join her. "Come over here."

Penny ran over to the bed and jumped into it next to her, pulling the quilt over her and her doll.

Tricia smiled. "Now, let's get some sleep. We both have school tomorrow, you know."

Penny hesitated.

"What, Pen?"

The six-year-old squinted at her. "I'm not sure Suzy can get to sleep good if she keeps thinking about ghosts."

"Oh. Right. Let me hold her for a second."

Penny handed her the doll. She rapidly mussed Suzy's artificial hair. "There. I scrubbed all the ghost stuff out of Suzy's mind."

"Does that work?"

"Would I do it if it didn't work? Now you need to get to sleep."

Her little sister's face dropped. "Oh—yeah…"

Tricia reached for the book that she had been reading earlier. "I'm gonna read some to wind down. You mind if I leave the light on for a little while?"

Tricia had never seen a smile appear so fast only to disappear just as quickly in a show of false bravado. "I don't care, but if you want to, go ahead."

She smiled and ruffled her sister's hair. "Just in case, you might be thinking about ghosts, too."

TWO

Still wearing the oversized T-shirt in which she slept, Tricia dragged herself into the dining room where her mother was cooking breakfast. She yawned and ran her fingers through the tangles of her light brown hair. "Ugh, what a mess."

"Don't know if you've heard, but there's this amazing new invention called a hairbrush," Mom said brightly. She looked past Tricia down the hall. "Where's your little sister?"

"She's coming."

Her mom was wearing her favorite tracksuit, baby blue with pink stripes that matched her pink running shoes. Her brown bangs were damp with sweat.

"You already ran?" Tricia asked.

"Why no, I've been sweating over a hot stove making pancakes for you people."

"Funny. So that's a yes."

She flexed her biceps. "Champ. Six miles on the dot."

Deadly Diet

"Katherine, where are my brown socks?" Dad yelled from the master bedroom upstairs.

"In the drawer, where they always are, Alan," Mom shouted, rolling her eyes.

"Never mind, they were in the drawer," Dad replied.

Mother and daughter smiled.

Mom flipped the pancakes. "Ever since we got here, your dad can't find his butt with both hands. I guess he's nervous about the promotion. There's a lot of responsibility in starting a new plant, and I think it's always on his mind." His new job as head of software development for Dynaco was the reason the Hall family had pulled up roots from Florida and moved to Bitterbrook, Oregon, a small town north of Portland on the other side of the Columbia River.

"Maybe he could get his old job back, then we could move back to Viera."

Her mother carried a platter of pancakes into the dining room and set them on the table next to a bowl of hash brown potatoes. "A return to Florida is not going to happen. Your dad loves his job and Portland is a great city. He just needs to realize how great he is at doing it. We can help him with that."

Tricia nodded. She sat in front of a plate of crispy hashed browns and a stack of pancakes painted with maple syrup for a touch of flavor—trying to watch the extra poundage like every other girl her age.

Penny skipped into the room, holding Suzy's hand, and sat at the white oak table. She licked chocolate from her fingers. Brown smudges stained the doll's dress. Tricia's little sister was built like a Pez candy dispenser—big head, thin body, only she loaded the candy into her mouth instead of dispensing it: Tootsie rolls, Goobers, Cheese Doodles, anything with a double-oh crazy name and a whole bunch of calories. The infuriating thing to Tricia was that Penny never gained any weight. The lucky little fat burner. Every candy bar, every snack Tricia ate took up residence on her thighs and butt.

"Ghosts are definitely not real," Penny declared, stamping her hand on the table, leaving a chocolate smudge.

"Penny, how many times have I told you not to eat candy before breakfast?" Mom scolded. She pulled a napkin from the holder and wiped her child's fingers and then the candy smear. "Wait. What was that about ghosts?"

"Oh, I said ghosts aren't real. Tricia scrubbed them out of my brains."

Her mom looked over at Tricia who smiled. "Yeah. We kinda had a thing with ghosts last night, but I took care of it."

"Glad to hear that. Now, Miss Penny, if I could just get your dad to stop giving you candy for cleaning your room. All those empty calories are bad for you. You're going to start putting on weight like ... crazy."

"Like me, you mean," Tricia said flatly.

Mom clucked her tongue. "No, not what I mean. But I'm also not going to stand here and tell you that you don't need to cut the crap from your diet."

"Here we go with the vegan arm twist."

"No arm twist, just a suggestion if you want to lose weight and feel healthier. Also save the planet and a few billion animals."

Dad came rushing into the dining room. He tied his yellow tie and kissed Mom on the cheek. "Veganism sucks and I'm late. Just give me a cup of coffee and one of those pancakes rolled around some blueberry jam."

Mom shook her head. "Alan, I made you this big breakfast and you don't even have time to eat it. Why can't you get up earlier? You could go jogging with me and do something for your health, while you're at it."

"No lectures, please, Kate, just the coffee and the roll thing. I'm gonna be late for a meeting."

Mom poured a cup of coffee into his portable mug. She handed him the cup and a rolled pancake. "Don't get blueberry on your shirt."

Dad frowned. "I won't."

"Hey, Dad," I said. "Five bucks says there will a blue polka dot on that yellow tie when you get home."

He sipped his coffee and smiled. "No bet."

"Hi, Daddly," Penny said around a mouthful of pancake.

Deadly Diet

"Hello and goodbye, Sweetling," Dad said. He pecked his trio of ladies on their cheeks. "Enjoy the vegan flapjacks and the tatery goodness. I'll see you all when I get home tonight. Oh, and I'll have steak with my baked potato and green item, please."

"In the fridge."

He kissed Mom again. "Love the vegan. Hate the veganism."

"Love the carnie. Hate the meat."

Dad flew out of the dining room as quickly as he had entered.

"The incredible vanishing man," Mom said shaking her head. "Except for his belly which seems to be expanding."

"That's mean. You think Dad will ever give up meats and eggs and cheese?" Tricia asked.

Mom sat and joined her daughters. "It's an uphill battle. Your Grams fed him a meat, a starch, a vegetable, and dessert every night until he left for college and she and your Gramps still eat that way. Unfortunately, they are both in their late 80's and still active as heck."

"You do realize what you just said? 'Unfortunately, they are active?' Wow. Sounds like you wish they both had heart disease."

"You know what I mean."

Mom was chill about what the family ate. Rather than force her vegan diet on them, she compromised by cooking lots of veggies, rice, and beans, while adding a few ounces of steak or pork chops or chicken as the main course for the infidels. Dessert always involved fruit, although Dad insisted on a variety of after-dinner snacks, both salty and sweet, to "enhance his television viewing experience."

Mom swallowed a bite of pancake. "I guess I don't mind the meat thing so much from a nutrition standpoint, but the sweet tooth he passed on to you and your sister makes me think of putting my foot down about sugary snacks."

"I wouldn't mind," Tricia lied.

Penny looked stricken. "You can't do it, Momsuds. Daddly says little kids can't live without sweet stuff."

"He also says that golf is a sport instead of people just standing there hitting a ball that doesn't move."

"It's kind of a strange arrangement the way we eat," Tricia said. "But I think it's pretty fair."

"It might seem fair, but that doesn't mean I like doing it. I just have to keep believing that one day, you all will come around to my way of thinking about food. Now, can you pass me the syrup?"

Tricia took a bite of potatoes and said, "What are you going to do today, Mom?"

"You know me. I can't sit still. Once I drop Penny off at kindergarten, I'm going to check out the local food co-op."

"What's that?"

"It's basically a grocery store owned by the people who shop there. They pick what the store stocks, where they get it, decide on the quality standards, plus they share in the profits. On our run this morning, Mrs. Alquist told me about the one near here after I told her why I do vegan."

"Sounds boring," Penny said.

Tricia ate another forkful. "What? The vegan lecture run or the communist grocery store?"

Mom cut her pancake into perfect forkfuls. "Very funny. You ready for your dance team tryout?"

"I guess. I know my routine backwards and forwards."

"Mrs. Alquist, Brynn's mom, says that all the girls at Bitterbrook want to be on the dance team. It's the 'dope' thing, as you all like to say, so it should be a great place for you to make some new friends."

"Nobody I know says dope anymore, but whatever," Tricia replied. Her phone buzzed. "Speaking of friends."

"Not at the table," Mom said. "Let it go to message."

"It's Megan and Mandy facetiming me before they go to class. Please, Mom."

"Go ahead. Just don't let your pancakes get too cold."

"I won't."

Tricia jumped up from the table, taking her plate with her and ran upstairs into her bedroom for privacy. She slid the onscreen button to green. Her friends appeared bunched together on the screen. Megan had changed her hair color from cherry red to neon blue and wore a retro *Dark Side of the Moon* T-shirt. Mandy had lost the nose ring, but now sported a hoop through her eyebrow. Her undercut hairstyle with shaved sides and longer hair on top was her latest attempt to stay on top of fashion. Her former squad was hanging in their spot at the courtyard of Viera High, a concrete bench near the Drama and Music Department. Tricia got a call back of her disquieting dream about her lost BFFs and the creepy zombie students from Bitterbrook.

"M and M's, what up, fam?" She took a bite of a pancake.

"You, Tee Riff," Megan said. "How're they hanging?"

She swallowed. "If you are referring to the girls, they are hanging fine. What's up with you dorklinquents?"

"Same shite. Different day. You?" Megan said.

"Trying out for the Bitterbrook High dance team, the Ravenettes."

"Dumb name, but okay. You're in," Megan said. Tricia didn't feel as confident as her friend did about her chances of making the team but appreciated Megan's faith in her.

"On to what's important," Mandy said. "What about guys?"

"Yeah, Tee. Any new prospects besides the Barf guy?"

"Everybody calls him Horf, and he is not a prospect. He's just a funny guy that I really like as a friend." She took another bite of her breakfast.

"What's his real name again?" Mandy asked.

"Harvey, Harv for short."

"That's almost as bad as Horf. What's up with that anyway?"

"When a stomach bug hits you in the middle of class and you decorate the teacher's shoes, the douchebags don't let you forget."

"So why is he not a prospect?" Megan asked. "I thought you said he was pretty chill."

Tricia ate the last piece of pancake. "He's not my type. Kind of soft and doughy. And you can't put soft and doughy types together with thick and chunky types."

"Yeah, you get mush," Megan said.

"But you said he makes you laugh and is easy to talk to," Mandy said.

"So is a TV set, Mando," Megan said. "She needs to find a guy like my Holder. The strong silent type. Big and dumb. Great kisser."

"Maybe she should just hook up with Frankenstein's monster," Mandy replied.

"Wow," Megan said. "Where did that reference come from?"

"British lit. We watched that old ass movie with Boris Lugosi or whatever."

Tricia laughed. "There is this guy, Trey, who sits behind me in math class, but I doubt he even knows I exist."

Mandy said, "Tee, I believe you can get any guy you want."

"But then she believes in the lizard people, so..." Megan said.

Mom rapped on her door and called, "Tricia, it's almost time to leave for school."

"I gotta roll," she said. "Later, dudettes." She blew her friends a kiss and pressed the red circle on her screen to hang up.

She squeezed into a pair of jeans and put on a loose powder blue sweater, her knee socks, and her grey lace-up sneaker boots. Onto the mangle of brown hair. After brushing out the snarls, she accented her eyes with mascara and dabbed on lip gloss. *Not a bad look. Understated, but alluring. Yeah, right, Tricia. You're a regular fashion plate.*

She shoved the black stretch pants and white tank top that her mother had bought her for the tryout into her backpack. Black and white were Bitterbrook High's school colors and Mom figured that it couldn't hurt to show a little school spirit. Tricia agreed. Now all she had to do was kill the same dance routine that had won first place on *Brevard's Got Talent*, the Florida county's homespun version of the network show, and no doubt she'd be in.

She slipped the backpack over her shoulders and bounded down the stairs.

Mom was helping Penny into her jacket.

"I'm leaving for the bus stop," Tricia said.

"Break a leg at the tryouts."

"Thanks, Mom."

"That's so mean. Why do you want her to break her leg?" Penny said. "Me and Suzy want her to be on the team."

"I don't really want her to break her leg, Penny..." Mom began to explain the old tradition of giving a performer good luck by wishing them bad. All Tricia had to say was break a leg with that.

Deadly Diet

She stepped outside onto the sidewalk and looked back at her Queen Anne style house. It didn't feel like it was "home" to her yet. It was too different from the Tuscany-influenced villa, with its open courtyard and balcony, where the Halls lived in Florida. The Oregon residence was what they called a foursquare because it has four rooms on both floors of the house. It was like a hundred years old, but well-built, at least that's what Dad says. To Tricia it felt like the owner dropped a farmhouse complete with a porch into a suburban lot. The Bitterbrook house felt like a relic from the past, perfect for haunting.

She looked up to gauge the late September weather. Troubling gray clouds hung in the sky, blocking out the sun and its warmth. *Was it going to rain again?* She almost went back into the house to grab her raincoat but feared she would miss the bus.

As she stood shivering at the bus stop, a plume of nasty smoke blew across her face. She turned and saw Brynn Alquist, the girl who lived down the street, standing next to her, smoking a cigarette. Tricia thought how stupid the Marlboro kill stick looked clenched in the teeth of such a pretty girl. Noxious fumes swirled around the smoker's stylish pixie cut and soaked her sweater in stink.

"What are you looking at, Trina?" Brynn said, smoke leaking from her teeth.

"Nothing. And it's Tricia."

"Tricia, Trina. Who gives a crap? You're friends with that creep Vomithorf."

Brynn's friend laughed. She, too, smoked a Marlboro and had her blonde hair styled in a perfectly snipped pixie cut. Two Bs in a pod.

Brynn blew smoke at Tricia. "Hey, Cathi, Trina here is trying out for the dance team today."

Cathi laughed. "Oh, really?"

"How do you know that?" Tricia asked.

"Duh. Our moms jog together. Doesn't yours bore you with the details of her life like mine or as I call her, my aunt's uncool sister."

"Uncool sister," Cathi chuckled. She took a drag on her cigarette.

"So, what if I am trying out?" Tricia asked. "What do you care?"

15

"I don't." Brynn snorted. She looked Tricia up and down, a judge at the county fair. "You really think you can make the team?"

"Yeah, I do."

Brynn leaned over and whispered something in Cathi's ear. They cracked up laughing.

Tricia ignored them.

The bus pulled up to the stop. Brynn took a last puff on her cigarette and blew more smoke her way. "Good luck, Trina," she said, flicking the butt at her. Cathi followed suit. The cackling friends stamped onto the bus and claimed the backseat.

Tricia glanced toward her house and recalled last night's episode with Penny and the doll. *Well, Pen. There may not be any ghosts in Bitterbrook, but I know of a couple of witches.*

She trudged up the steps of the bus and took a seat at the front as far away from Brynn and Cathi as possible.

When they arrived at school and she got off the bus, she saw Trey Curtis among the bustling crowd of students and her stomach did a backflip. He was tall and muscular, the stud on the swim team. His hair was a luscious pile of curls, buzzed short on the sides. You could tell he was a swimmer because his hair had just the slightest tinge of green from the chlorine. Trey reminded her of a non-tanned version of the Florida boys that she and her friends used to drool over at Viera High.

As she walked past him, she tried to say hi, but the word stuck in her throat.

"Yo, Tricia!"

She turned and saw Horf White walking toward her. He wore a baggy T-shirt, skinny jeans that were a tad tight for his ample frame and a pair of black Doc Martens boots. The picture on his T-shirt was that of the iconic Chinese Communist, Mao Zedong. The Chairmen's face was bleeding, and his famous blue jacket was shredded by claws. The caption read, "In Waking a Tiger, Use a Long Stick."

"How was your weekend, Horf?"

"You know how I told you I don't get along with my dad at all. Well, yesterday, he dragged me on our usual hunting trip, and told me that he's divorcing my mom and wanted to know if I was going to miss him. I said, are you kidding? At this range?"

16

Deadly Diet

The deadpan expression on his face made her chuckle. In all the time she had known him, she had never seen him laugh at one of his own jokes.

"Hey, I got a favor to ask you," she said.

"What's that?"

"I was wondering if you'd come with me to dance team tryouts."

He shook his head. "Can't do it. I have to work this afternoon."

"Work? Since when? You always told me that work was a poor way to make money."

"I got a job at the Cornucopia market. Remember? I told you I want to build a badass gaming computer, so I can dedicate myself to turning pro in *Trigger Fingers from Hell*."

"Oh, yeah. I forgot. You're going to become a millionaire by playing in first person shooter tournaments."

"Winning first person shooter tournaments. I start this afternoon... at the market... not on becoming a legend."

"Is Cornucopia that food co-op my mom was talking about this morning?"

"Hardly, it's owned by the capitalist overlord Grunion."

"Too bad. I was hoping you could throw a banana peel on the floor while Brynn Alquist was dancing."

"I would prefer to toss a grenade," Horf said. He held up a finger and then put his phone to his mouth. "I meant green egg. Do you hear that Deep State beeyocrats? I meant toss a green egg."

Tricia laughed. "You're sure you won't blow off your first day at work for me?"

He nodded. "Although I find the whole idea of being a drudge for the bougies to be distasteful, I need the money. You're on your own."

Tiny yikes. She was going to have to face the tryouts all by her lonesome. She hoped she would be up to the task.

THREE

When Tricia arrived at the gym for the auditions, she was completely unprepared for what they were really like. Heated air blew from three noisy giant fans. The unpleasant warmth was stifling. The synthetic smell of the rubber mats made her queasy. The dance team coach Mary Milton was a stocky woman with muscular calves so big technically they were cows. Even though she didn't have a mustache, it seemed that she should, hence her nickname "Mustache Milton." She stood with her clipboard in hand, pen at the ready to mark down any flubs. At least thirty dancers were there, and all of them were beautiful and in great shape. Girls stretched and warmed up on mats, doing backflips and splits. Tricia was surprised to see guys from the basketball team standing around, hooting, and flirting with the hopefuls. It was a circus, and all of a sudden, she was the fat lady. Without her Florida friends to back her up, her confidence wilted.

She wanted to bolt, but when she saw Brynn and Cathi sucking up to the coach, she decided she couldn't let them hold her cowardice over her head for the rest of the year. Brynn spotted her and tapped Cathi on the shoulder. She pointed at Tricia, and they shared an exaggerated giggle.

Tricia trudged up the bleachers to take a seat where some other girls were waiting. She overheard a couple of them talking.

"I got the fat on my thighs sucked out with liposuction this summer," the redheaded girl said. She was a rail.

"For reals? I would kill to get the fat sucked off me." Her friend looked like a runway model.

Rail said, "My legs got bruised up and it hurt like hell, but it was worth it to look right for the team. I hear we're going to compete in D.C. again, if we win the district."

"Awesome," Runway said. "Go, Ravenettes."

Yikes.

"Everybody, listen up," Mustache Milton announced gruffly, stampeding a herd of horseflies in Tricia's stomach. "I am going to call out your name. You will either give us an audition tape or we will play our standard dance piece. You will have two minutes to do your routine, so make it good."

Tricia took a deep breath and corralled her rampaging nerves.

"Kelly Williams, you're first," Mustache Milton said.

The dancer formerly known as Rail bounced to the middle of the mat. Her toothy white grin was a neon sign that advertised "perky." The rhythmic Latin beat of congas started to pound the gym walls. As Kelly performed a precise flawless salsa, the boys in the peanut gallery cheered and whistled. Tricia got the sudden feeling that she had made a bad mistake being there. These lean, lit girls were too much competition for her. She felt like a fat, ugly clunk. How could she have been so stupid to think that she could just walk in, do a little dance number, and make the team?

She wanted to flee the gym and keep running all the way home but felt too self-conscious to move. Everyone would know that she'd chickened out, especially Brynn. She'd be teased unmercifully by the head of the coven and her witchy followers. Tricia desperately wanted to call Megan and Mandy for a pep talk filled with reassurances about her dancing abilities, but knew they still were in class and couldn't answer their phones.

An Asian girl with flowing black hair walked alone into the gymnasium. Tricia recognized her from her fourth-period gym class. Her name was Tomoko. She was an exchange student from Japan. There was a sadness about her reflected in her brown eyes. She wondered what a pretty girl like her had to be sad about, especially one with such a tiny waist and such slim hips. Maybe she, too, was feeling intimidated by the crowd of gawkers judging all of them. Tomoko sat alone in the top row of the bleachers.

Tricia turned her attention to a new dancer who was starting her routine. She was another thin blonde, too good to miss making the team.

She thought the first and second girls were locks until she saw competitor number three dance. This girl should have been on television. Her routine was full of spiraling jumps and spins. Each time she took flight, she landed perfectly on the beat. The boys let go with a chorus of hoots and high-five slaps. The horseflies again stampeded in Tricia's belly.

A sense of observation drew her attention. She turned. The Japanese exchange student was staring at her. When their eyes met, she turned quickly away. Weird.

"Okay. Brynn Alquist, you're next," Mustache Milton called.

Brynn walked out, waving to the crowd as if it were filled with her fans, before starting her routine. Tricia hoped her tormentor would trip and fall. She didn't. Brynn wasn't the best of the dancers, but her charisma and sex appeal made up for her lack of precision. The boys whistled and called her name. When she was done, she barely had broken a sweat.

"Nailed it, Brynn," Mustache Milton said with a familiarity that suggested Brynn was a shoe-in. The coach read silently down her list and prepared to announce the next name. Tricia's stomach tingled.

Not me. Not yet. Please, not me, not yet.

"Cathi Metcalf," she yelled.

Brynn's BFF sprang from the bleachers and ran on her toes to the center of the gym floor. She crouched before exploding with a spread-eagle jump into the air to begin her high energy routine. *What the hell! Is this a regular high school or a freaking dance academy?*

Tricia was surprised when Tomoko stepped down onto the bleacher where she was sitting and joined her. "Do you mind if I sit here? I am feeling nervous," she said. Her English was measured and exact, with just a trace of an accent. She smiled with perfect white teeth.

"No problem. I'm kind of nervous myself. Tomoko, right?"

The girl nodded.

"What song are you doing?" She asked.

"*Girl Be Dancing* by Kitty Nibbles. Very popular at home."

"Where in Japan are you from?"

"I am from Kamakura. It is a beach town an hour south of Tokyo."

"I'm a beach girl, too. I used to live on the coast in Florida near the Space Center, so my friends and I always went to Cocoa Beach. How did you end up at Bitterbrook?"

"When I was twelve, my grandfather moved to Portland to curate a new history museum dedicated to Asian cultures. We were very close. When I reached high school, I became an exchange student to be with him again. But my parents did not want me to stay with Grandfather who lived in Old Town. They told me that it was a bad neighborhood, but I believe it was because it was also called Chinatown and Father does not like the Chinese. So, I applied to school here and stayed with the Henderson family. I visit Grandfather on the weekends when I can."

"How do you like Bitterbrook?" Tricia asked.

"Much rain, but I like the change in seasons. Most satisfying."

"Not a fan. Town's kind of small for me, too."

Mustache Milton called out the next name. "Patricia Hall."

Tomoko said, "Kamakura was once the fourth largest city in the world."

"In the world?"

"Yes. In the 13th Century."

Tricia laughed.

"Patricia Hall, we're waiting."

She jolted. "Oh, what?"

Mustache Milton waved her clipboard toward the floor. "Anytime, Patricia."

What was it with this place and getting her name wrong? She smiled weakly and stood. Her knees started to shake. "Uh, it's Tricia."

"You have a song, or you want the default?"

She held up her phone.

"Get to it then."

Tricia took a deep breath, steadied herself, and walked in a way that best approximated confidence. She handed her phone to another stocky gym teacher, Assistant Coach Higgs, AKA Mini-Milt since she was shorter than Coach Milton but just as gruff. Mini-Milt linked her phone to the Bluetooth speakers and gave Tricia a thumbs up.

She moved to the middle of the floor. She heard a snicker and knew who it was. Mini-Milt quieted Brynn with a violent shush.

"Okay, Patricia, you've got two minutes," Mustache announced.

"It's Tricia, Coach."

"Right. Two minutes, Tricia, and you just burned a couple of seconds."

She nodded to Assistant Coach Higgs who pressed play on her phone. The music began, and she started her routine to the disco-pop song *Uptown Funk*.

On the first beat, she did a split and then bounced up into a series of robotic moves. As she danced, she felt liberated. She could feel the music driving away the nervousness in her stomach. She leapt and did a spinning pirouette. She was on, hitting every move right on the beat. Five years of lessons had paid off. She couldn't stop a big smile from blossoming on her cheeks. She executed a leaping split. Her arms raised in exultation. She expected to hear applause raining down on her. "Thunder thighs," one of the basketball players hooted. Laughter followed.

Her ears burned and her head spun. She stumbled into the next move.

"Sooey," another boy called. Mustache Milton turned and glared at him.

Tricia didn't remember much of what happened after that. She reeled through the rest of her routine. Her face was on fire with

22

embarrassment. After she was done, Mustache Milton muttered something about "nice routine," but all Tricia heard was "thunder thighs" and "sooey" and the mocking laughter that had followed. She made it to the locker room before she burst into tears.

She stumbled into the sickening smell of stale socks, sweaty towels, and chlorine from the shower disinfectant. She felt humiliated, alone, dejected, incompetent, the fattest hog in the world. She couldn't escape her image in the array of mirrors above the line of shared sinks. Mascara streaked from her damp eyes and ran down her cheeks. The fabric of her leggings pressed against her thighs, and she realized how big her ham hocks really were. She saw herself for who she was—not the hundred-pound seventh grader who had aced the talent contest, but the five foot-two, one-hundred-and-forty-five-pound sow who had just humiliated herself in front of all those people.

She trudged to her locker and got dressed. She wanted to throw the stupid black-and-white outfit in the trash but shoved it into her backpack. She took a quick shower and put on her street clothes. She was about to leave when the door to the locker room opened. It was Tomoko.

"Where did you go?" she asked. "I wanted to tell you I thought you were very good."

"Yeah, right." Tricia sighed.

"I do not understand. Your dancing was excellent."

"For a sow, didn't you hear them calling sooey? Sooey is how farmers call pigs. Get it? Isn't that funny?"

"It is not so funny."

"I don't know what ever made me think I could make the team. I knew that I didn't have a prayer when I saw all those hot, skinny girls. Look at me. I'm a—thunder thighs."

Tricia vomited a hot sob. She reached into her backpack and grabbed an energy bar. She tore off the wrapper and took a huge bite of sugary comfort, tasting salty tears as well.

Tomoko gasped and looked away from her. Tricia guessed such emotional outbursts as hers were undignified in her culture. *So what?*

Mini-Milt stuck her head into the locker room and yelled, "Coach wants everybody out here. She's announcing the team." The clueless assistant closed the door unaware of her distress.

Tricia didn't move. She took a big bite of the power bar. "Sorry. You want a piece?"

Tomoko looked at the floor and shook her head. "You are not going?"

"Why bother?" She took another huge bite finishing the bar. "There's no way I made it." She dabbed at her tears with the sleeves of her sweater, not caring about the black stains from the mascara. "

"You did very well until you stumbled. What if you make the team and you are not there to hear? They will think you do not want to be on the team. Please, we can stand by the door together. I think you will be happy and surprised." She smiled sweetly.

Tricia licked chocolate off her fingers. She was trapped by the possibility of the long shot coming in. She followed Tomoko to the exit door.

"I want to thank all the girls who came out," Mustache Milton boomed. "You know we can't take everyone on the team, and if you didn't make it this year, there's always next year. And now I want these girls to join me."

The coach called out the names of the fifteen girls who had made the team. To Tricia, each announcement was a punch and a body blow. Cathi's name was a right hook, her smirk was a crowing I-told-you-so. Tomoko's name was a jab, her smile an apology.

"And the last girl …"

Tricia tensed, still harboring the slightest of hopes of making the team.

"… Brynn Alquist." Mustache Milton said, delivering the knockout punch.

Tricia stepped away from the door, letting it close.

"I do not understand. You were very good," Tomoko said, unintentionally kicking her while she was down.

Tricia clenched her fist and slammed it against her thigh. "Next semester is going to be different. I swear I'm going to get serious about losing all this disgusting flab. No more pigging out on junk food, no more fried crap at lunch, no more sitting on her giant butt in front of the television. I swear to God, I'm going to get thin or die trying."

She thought she saw just the hint of a smile appear on Tomoko's face, but it was so sudden it could have been a nervous twitch. "I must go to join the dance team," the Japanese girl said. "We will talk later." She turned away from her and ran out the door, leaving her to wonder, talk about what?

FOUR

"You haven't touched a thing on your plate, Tricia. Are you still upset about not making the dance team?" Mom asked her at the dinner table.

Tricia cranked up a weak smile. "I'm not hungry."

"Honey, life's full of disappointments," Dad said. "You have to be able to deal with them." He stuffed a slab of juicy beef into his mouth. "Now, eat."

"I said I'm not hungry."

"You tried your best, didn't you?" Dad asked.

She nodded. A lump came to her throat. Tears lurked behind her eyes.

"Well, then, you have nothing to be ashamed of. Now, eat your dinner before it gets cold." He nodded toward her food.

She stabbed a piece of steak with her fork, then dropped it back onto the plate. A tear slid down her cheek. She wiped it away before anyone could see it.

"Tricia, we don't waste food. Eat," he said.

26

Deadly Diet

She exploded in tears and frustration. "Damn it, Dad! Leave me alone about the stupid food. I didn't make the team because I'm too fat. Don't you get it? I didn't make it because I'm a Porky Piggette!"

Penny giggled at the funny name.

Tricia pushed away from the table, ran up the stairs and into her room. She jumped on the bed and buried her face in her pillow. She sobbed until she thought her heart would burst.

Her mother walked into the room and sat on the bed next to her.

"Tricia, I want to talk to you."

"Go away," she cried miserably.

"Just for a minute, and then I'll leave you alone." Her soft voice highlighted her concern.

Tricia paused and then nodded. Mom stroked her hair. "Did your coach tell you that the reason you didn't make the team was because you were too... overweight?"

"You mean too fat, don't you?"

"No," she said calmly. "I want to know if the coach told you that was the reason you didn't make the team, because if she did, I'm going to have a little talk with her and her principal." An undercurrent of anger hardened her mother's voice.

"She didn't say it that way," Tricia said.

Thunder thighs!

"Then what made you think that?"

Sooey!

"Tricia, I'd like an answer."

"Look at me, Mom. I'm fat. Face it. All the girls who made the team were thin and pretty."

"You're not fat. A hundred and thirty-five pounds is not that big."

"A hundred and forty-five pounds, Mom."

"Still not that big."

"Then why are you always trying to get me to go running with you and quit eating junk food?"

"I want you to be healthy."

"Come on. You don't think I'm fat?"

Mom hesitated. "You might need to lose a few of the pounds you put on last summer."

"Like I said, fat."

Mom sighed. "If you really don't like where you're at weight-wise, you can do something about it."

"I'm going to. Starting tomorrow morning, I'm doing your vegan thing full on, and I'm not stopping until I'm down to where I want to be."

"Doing the 'vegan thing' isn't going to automatically make you lose weight. You can still pig out on rice and cookies and muffins. You have to eat when you're hungry, not when you're bored or sad or whatever. And if you do it sensibly, you're probably not going to lose weight fast."

"Wait. So, you think I'm overeating because I'm sad and bored?" *Because you would be exactly right.*

"That's not what I'm saying. I'm saying you have to do things smart and not try to lose weight as fast as you can. It took time to put the extra weight on, it's going to take about the same amount of time to take the extra weight off."

"I'm not a complete idiot, Mom. I know my thighs didn't get ginormous overnight."

"Your 'ginormous' thighs are perfectly fine. Anyway, I just don't want you to get impatient if you don't lose the weight as fast as you think you should."

"I won't. Oh, and I want you to wake me up early tomorrow morning so I can go running with you."

"Seriously?"

"I mean it. Wake me and make me get up. No excuses."

"No excuses. But one thing. I want you to promise me that you won't go on any of those crazy diets if you don't lose weight like you think you should."

"I promise. I'm going to lose weight the old-fashioned way. Diet pills and cigarettes."

"Funny. Now come back downstairs and help clear the table."

FIVE

Later that night, Tricia lay in bed reliving the pain and humiliation of the tryouts. She pondered how the awesome feeling that she was nailing the audition had twisted into such hurt that she felt hollowed out. She had even lied in her texts to Megan and Mandy telling them that she had made the team and been named a co-captain to spare her from their well-meaning sympathy. Big mistake. Their enthusiastic comebacks confirming their confidence in her made her feel much worse about herself than the truth would have, since she was now a loser and a liar. She needed something to make her feel better and the thought of eating a root beer float loaded with vanilla ice cream and topped with whipped cream and a cherry popped into her head. A small one, coffee cup sized. Just a gulp, really. She squinted at the clock on her nightstand and saw that it was past two-thirty. *That's just what you need to do at this hour, Tricia, trade a moment of sweet pleasure for a lump of sugary badness that will sit on your gut for the rest of the night.* She closed her eyes and tried to get back to sleep.

The vanilla ice cream in the freezer called her. *Hey, Tricia, I can make you feel better about being a lying loser. All you need do is plop me into a glass of frothy root beer and top me off with whipped cream and a cherry, then down the hatch for a dose of sweet, sweet consolation. Come downstairs and make it happen.*

She flipped over onto her side, turning away from the door.

Come on, girl. We're so yummy. And you're so sad. Let's do this thing.

She pulled the sheet and blanket up around her head to wrap her in a cocoon of inaction. She closed her eyes and tried to think of something that would lull her to sleep.

She pictured herself lying on a blanket at her favorite spot at Cocoa Beach. Megan and Mandy lay next to her, soaking up the rays. The surf crashed rhythmically in the background. Surfers cut across the waves offshore, throwing up sprays of saltwater. She slathered herself with sunscreen that smelled like vanilla ice cream. All around her, tourists with white zinc noses and dumb hats popped the tops on cans of root beer. As the surfers glided to shore into the whipped cream foam, they pointed at her and made fat faces by puffing their cheeks. The girls sitting on beach towels around her, giggled and tossed cherries at her. Sea gulls shrieked and dove for the cherries plucking them off the hot sand and her flesh.

Tricia opened her eyes unsure of whether she had fallen asleep and dreamed of the unpleasant scene at the beach or just imagined it.

The ice cream and the root beer called her from the refrigerator again. *We're still waiting for you to do what we know you're going to do. Do you want to feel better or not, you fibbing failure? We can't wait here all night while you delay the inevitable.*

She pulled the blanket down from her head and stared at the ceiling as if a note about willpower was written there. It wasn't. She swung her legs onto the cold floor. Her bare feet searched for her slippers with tippy tap toes. She found them and pulled them toward her. She slid each foot into the upper vamp of a slipper.

In her mind, she heard Brynn's cackling laughter and the hog calls of the boys in the gym. *Sooey. Sooey.* She set her jaw and kicked the slippers off her feet, sending them flying across the room. "No," she said banging back onto the bed. She shoved her feet under the blanket and pulled it up to her neck. There will be no late-night snacks tonight. She closed her eyes and smiled. Her stomach realized that it had lost and growled.

But one victorious battle of the bulge did not win a war. She had a long struggle ahead of her and tonight's triumph would be short lived.

SIX

It seemed like Tricia had just fallen back to sleep when she heard her mother's soft singsong call: "Tricia, time to get up." She opened an eye and saw that it was still dark outside. She closed it and drifted back to sleep.

"Tricia, wake up!" Her mother's insistent voice startled her. "You said you wanted to go running no matter what, and I don't want Mrs. Alquist waiting on us."

Groggily, she sat up in bed, squinting at her mother's silhouette framed by the light coming from the hallway. Mom was already dressed and ready to go. Tricia looked out the window into the cold darkness, then glanced at the clock. It was 5:30 A.M.

"You sounded pretty determined last night," Mom said. "You still want to go?"

She mumbled a reply.

"Was that yes?"

She slapped her thighs. "Yeah, that's a yes."

Deadly Diet

She dragged her feet out of the bed and put them on the cold floor. She withdrew them and asked her mother to toss her a pair of socks.

She slipped her socks on and hurried into the bathroom. After she was done, she dressed quickly and followed Mom downstairs and out the front door.

It felt wrong to be up so early, against everything intelligent teenagers stood for. Shivering on the porch, Tricia waited for her mother to lock the door. According to her phone, the temperature was a brisk 54 degrees. The chill in the air gnawed the lingering sleepiness off her bones. With glowing yellow eyes, the darkened streets watched her pat her arms and rock back and forth from foot to foot, trying to get warm. The eerie stillness of the neighborhood left her with a sense that her mother and she were the only ones left on earth.

"Okay, first we stretch and then we go," Mom said. "Mrs. Alquist is waiting for us at the end of the block." She touched her toes. I did the same, glad to be doing something to get the warm blood flowing at the start of her journey to the land of slim.

She and her mother found Mrs. Alquist doing squat thrusts under the streetlight on the corner. Brynn's mother looked as though she was expecting company and not a sweaty run. Her blonde hair was perfectly styled in a short blunt bob. Her running outfit, blue satin with a white reflective stripe, matched her shoes. Tricia wasn't surprised to see that she had taken the time to put on makeup.

"I see we have a new member of our little running club," Mrs. Alquist said. "Good. Good. The more the merrier."

"More like misery loves company," Mom said. "Right, Tricia?"

"Funny. Can we just go?"

"We can."

As they jogged, Tricia was thankful that Mrs. Alquist hadn't brought up her failure to make the dance team. Brynn must have told her, but Mrs. Alquist had chosen to remain silent. Nice lady. Crap daughter.

After three blocks, the moms were barely puffing. Tricia, on the other hand, was dribbling snot from her nose and had a bad case of strep throat from sucking in the cold air. Those trifles were nothing compared to the swarm of stinging caterpillars that had hatched in her thighs and itched like crazy. She clenched her teeth, and in the growing light of dawn, counted the cracks in the sidewalk to keep her mind off the maddening itch.

She kept going, hoping that the tingling caterpillars would stop. They didn't.

She picked up her pace, believing that an increase in circulation would carry the itch away. Wrong. The irritation kicked it up a notch, becoming an unrelenting prickling that she tried to relieve by scraping her skin with her fingernails.

Her mother and Mrs. Alquist jogged ahead of her, oblivious to her discomfort.

She dug her nails into her sweatpants and scratched the affected area as if scraping bark from a pine tree. The itching would not stop.

So, she did. "Mom! Hold up!"

Her mother turned and jogged back to join her. Mrs. Alquist followed.

"What's wrong, Tricia?" Mom asked.

"I can't keep going. My legs are itching like crazy," she groaned, furiously scratching her thighs. "What's going on?"

"Runner's itch. If you've had a long time between running sometimes the blood vessels expand, causing a sensation that your brain reads as itchiness. The cold doesn't help."

"But how do you make it go away?"

"Unfortunately, you have to work through it."

"Work through it? Oh my God, I can't take it."

Mrs. Alquist said, "The itching will get better as you build up stamina."

"Shit," Tricia hissed. "I mean shoot."

Mom let her slip of the tongue go. "Come on, honey, we'll powerwalk for a little and see if that helps."

She nodded and copied her mother's arm-pumping, almost-running stride. She was glad no one was on the street to see her doing this dumbass duck walk.

As the itch lessened from maximum aggravation to minor annoyance, she observed the town around her. The rising sun made the woods on the horizon glow as if a fire were approaching them from behind. The streets were quiet except for the occasional bark of a dog. A couple of cars rumbled past them. Lights winked on inside houses, signaling the awakening of the occupants. An old lady, wrapped in a robe and wearing galoshes, trundled from porch to driveway to retrieve her newspaper. A man dressed for work in a long-sleeved oxford shirt and khaki pants dragged his trash can to the curb. Bitterbrook was rising from the dead of night.

As they pushed past the Henderson's house, Tricia looked up at a second-story bedroom window. Tomoko Tanaka gazed from the darkness of her room, deep in thought. Tricia waved to her, but she didn't return her greeting. Tomoko seemed anxious. She brought her cupped hand toward her mouth as if she were about to eat a handful of peanuts. Suddenly, she stopped moving. Her eyes widened with apparent fear. Slowly, she looked behind her. It was as if she had been caught doing something that she wasn't supposed to be doing, which was just too weird for words. Tomoko threw whatever was in her hand across the room and backed away from the window. Someone shut the curtains.

The disturbing encounter left Tricia feeling uncomfortable and a little concerned for the exchange student. Was it possible that Mr. or Mrs. Henderson was being abusive to Tomoko? Was that why she seemed so scared? It seemed unlikely that the beloved Mr. Henderson, a math teacher at Bitterbrook High affectionately known as Hendo, or his equally respected wife Midge who worked at the local church, were abusers of a teenager placed in their care, but something had just scared Tomoko. Tricia just didn't know at the time who or, should I say, what it was.

SEVEN

When Tricia got to school, she was dying for something, anything, to eat that wasn't oatmeal and applesauce, the concoction that her mother had made her for her breakfast that morning. Starving people in China would've had a hard time choking down that gunk. In contrast, Penny and her dad had enjoyed bite after bite of syrup-smothered French toast and crispy sausage links. Tricia waited until her mom went to get a second cup of matcha tea before she snagged a link, shushing her sister with a threatening look.

As she hustled up the stairs, she munched on the savory sausage, enjoying every morsel. When she was done, guilt slammed her. One day—no—one morning on her diet, and she was already cheating. Shaking her head in disgust, she trudged into the bathroom, squeezed a blob of toothpaste onto her brush and scrubbed away the taste of sage and shame.

This was going to be harder than I thought.

Now, here she was standing next to her locker near the cafeteria and all she could smell was food cooking: the savory aroma of

Deadly Diet

Salisbury steak, the sweet smell of peach cobbler, the yeasty scent of baking bread. She opened the brown bag that her mom had packed for her and ate a carrot that was supposed to be part of her lunch. It tasted alright but did nothing to curb her appetite. She began to regret going down the rabbit hole with her. She wanted something sweet to eat, something like …

Horf.

In one hand he held a powdered-sugar-coated doughnut; in the other, a small bag containing more of the sweet treats.

… Something like that.

Horf stopped at her locker and said, "Fun fact. Did you know the naked mole rat practices coprophagy?"

"I try to limit my knowledge about naked mole rats to nothing. Can I have a bite of that?" Tricia asked. A small bite of donut would take the edge off her hunger.

"Coprophagy means they eat their own feces. Isn't that weird?"

"Not as weird as your telling me about it first thing in the morning. Now can I have a bite?"

"Sure." He handed her the doughnut. "Knowledge is power, am I right? You never know when you might run into a starving mole rat enraged by a bad case of constipation."

She took a nibble. The powdery sugar tasted so good she wanted to inhale the whole thing.

"You can have the rest," Horf said. "In the words of Chris P. Cream, my donut is your donut."

"Better not," she said, taking another bite. "I'm trying to lose these." She slapped her thighs.

"Hard to run from a constipated, enraged mole rat without legs. Kind of an essential body part for getting around."

"I'm talking about these thunder thighs."

"What the hell? Your thighs aren't that big."

"The dance team's judges didn't think so," she said.

"Seriously, you really care what they think? The system's rigged ahead of time anyway. The same girls make it every year."

"Next semester, I'll be one of them. I'm gonna be so thin, they're gonna beg me to be on the team." She banged her hand on her locker.

Horf jumped. "What the frick, Tricia?"

"Damn it," she snapped.

"What's wrong?"

She showed him the powdered sugar clinging to her fingers. "I just ate the whole stupid doughnut you gave me."

"Uh, you asked me for it."

"You should have told me no."

"Okay, no."

"I'm serious. I'm really trying to lose weight. I can't have my friends undermining me."

Horf scoffed. "Undermining you? How the hell am I supposed to know you're on a fricking diet?"

She saw the hurt look on his face. "I'm sorry, Horf. It's not your fault I'm a pig. I just can't stop thinking about food and it's only the first day of my diet."

"You don't need to lose weight for those dance-holes. You look great to me."

"You're a majority of one."

"What kind of diet are you on anyway?"

"Vegan. My mom gave me a book." She reached into her backpack and handed the book to her friend.

He read the cover. "Venture into Veganism. It must be thorough. I mean lots of thought went into the title." He flipped through the pages of vegetable-based dishes in the book. "You know what this is, don't you?"

"What?"

"A recipe book for disaster. What teenager in their right mind is going to give up burgers and fries and sweet stuff for tofu and cauliflower?"

"I know, right, but I have to do something about my flab." She wiped the powder off her pants and took the book from him. "I don't need this..." She crammed the book into her backpack. "What I need is willpower."

"You can get that at the school supply store," Horf said. "It's next to the pencils."

"Thanks for the heads up. I'm gonna give this veggie thing a try, but if it doesn't work, I'll do whatever it takes to lose weight."

"Just don't go all bulimic on me and start eating bags of cookies then barfing them up. We don't need another kid at this school nicknamed for regurgitation. Although Barf Hall would be a good name for a gameshow host."

She smiled. "We'd better get to class."

They headed in opposite directions.

"Hey, Tricia," Horf said, turning back toward her. "I mean it when I say don't get all weird about losing weight. Anorexia and bulimia and stuff like that can kill you."

"I'm not gonna go anorexic or bulimic."

"Promise?"

"I promise. Once I get to where I want to be, I'll stop dieting and maintain my weight."

Horf smiled. "Good. I wouldn't want you to end up being a walking skeleton."

"Don't worry, I won't."

EIGHT

By the time fourth-period gym class arrived, Tricia's hunger was a relentless demon raking her insides with dull claws to make room for something to eat. Outside the locker room was a snack machine full of candies, cookies, potato chips, pretzels, and granola bars, a treasure trove of temptation. The dispenser of delicious delights rattled with the sound of dropping coins. A tall kid in jeans and a black T-shirt pushed the selection buttons and a slab of milk chocolate dropped into the retrieval bin. The boy shoved his hand through the door of the bin and retrieved the bar of goodness. He peeled off the wrapper and snapped off a thick chunk with his teeth. A slight smile of satisfaction expressed his opinion of the candy's sweet taste.

In her head, she tried to list the merits of eating an apple.

A seventh grader, all pigtails and freckles, put her change in the machine and ran her finger along the glass front until she settled on a yellow bag of M&Ms with peanuts. She pushed the appropriate buttons, but the bag didn't drop. It hung by a snippet of wrapper. She banged on the glass front of the machine, but the bag remained suspended between expectation and fulfilment.

"Stupid thing," the little girl grumbled. She left the bag hanging and stormed off.

"OMG," Tricia whispered. The girl's choice of candy and the failure of the vending machine to deliver it to her had to be a cosmic message from the Great Beyond of Florida, Megan and Mandy's way of helping her out. Those M & Ms were meant for her. And as a bonus, peanuts were nutritious. She would just peel off the candy and chocolate and eat the nuts.

Sure, Tricia. And Trey Curtis is going to ask you out tonight.

She hustled over to the snack dispenser. The bag was ready to fall. She looked around for witnesses. The coast was clear. She pressed against the glass face, lifting the machine several inches from the ground. She let it go. It banged loudly, rocking slightly forward. The bag stayed.

"Damn," she whispered under her breath.

She lifted the machine again a little higher and let go.

The dispenser landed hard and rocked forward farther than it had the time before. She quickly steadied it. She didn't want to win a Darwin award for being crushed to death by a candy machine that she accidentally rocked on top of her. She looked. The retrieval bin was still empty.

Chewing her bottom lip when she should have been chewing candy-coated peanuts, she pressed her hands against the upper face of the vending machine and loaded up her arms and legs to give it one last shove. She lifted the dispenser off the ground before letting it drop, keeping her hands on the glass face to push back if need be. The machine rocked toward her, and she was barely able to stop it. She grunted and set it back into place, her heart suddenly pumping faster. *Maybe this wasn't such a good idea...*

And then the bag of M&Ms dropped into the bin.

"Yes," she hissed, pumping her fist. She reached into the bin and grabbed the candies.

"Hey, those are mine!"

She turned and saw the little girl who had purchased the candy walking toward her with Mini-Milt Higgs in tow.

Tricia changed color and shrank to the size of a red M&M. "I'm sorry. I thought… I – I didn't know you were coming back."

The girl put her hands on her hips and replied, "I got Coach Higgs to give me my money back or open the machine to get my M&Ms and you stole them."

Mini-Milt shook her head. "We don't need people banging up the machines. How do you think they get broken in the first place?"

"I'm sorry," she said sheepishly.

"Gimme my candy," the girl replied sticking out her hand.

Tricia forked over the bag to her. "Sorry."

Out of the corner of her eye, she saw some of the girls who had made the dance team, Brynn and Cathi among them, laughing at her.

"I'd better not catch you shoving our machines again," Mini-Milt said. "Breaking a thousand-dollar machine for a sixty-five-cent bag of candy doesn't make much sense, does it?"

She nodded, realized her mistake, and corrected it by shaking her head in the negative.

The smirking Brynn said something to the other girls. Her friends puffed up their cheeks and curved their arms to simulate fat bodies. Her ears burned.

The assistant coach marched toward the locker room, ordering the other girls to get ready for class. She turned back to her and held her palms up as if she were a human scale. "A thousand-dollar machine, sixty-five cents worth of candy, not an even trade."

Tricia nodded and waited until Mini-Milt was safely ensconced in her office before she followed her into the locker room to dress for gym. She opened her locker and put her backpack in it. The M&M incident revealed how much sweets controlled her behavior in a bad way. The irony was that her being exposed as a pig and a thief made her long for the comfort that sweets provided. She dropped onto the bench and started getting undressed. A gurgling growl startled her. For once, her stomach wasn't the culprit. It was Tomoko Tanaka dressed for class in her grey Bitterbrook gym shirt and black shorts. Her eyes were puffy as if she had been up all night. She looked exhausted.

Deadly Diet

"How are you this morning, Tricia? You are still not upset about failing to make the dance team."

"No, but thanks for bringing it up." She slipped on her grey T-shirt.

"I am sorry. I was thinking about you last night."

"Thinking about me?"

A box of cellophane-wrapped Scooter Pies came flying over the top of the row of lockers. It hit the floor and broke open, spilling the round, marshmallow-filled pies.

Tomoko cried out and jumped back from the exploding box.

The box startled Tricia, too, but only for a second.

"Someday I'm gonna make Brynn sorry she ever messed with me," she said, scooping the pies up and tucking them back into the box. Tomoko was in a panic. For a moment she thought that she was going to run.

"Hey, Trina, you like the flying Scooter Pies?"

She turned to see Brynn Alquist strutting around the corner of the lockers.

"Yeah, they were great, Brynn. I ate all of them," she said.

"Mom told me about you joining the morning jog and how you were trying to lose weight. Just wanted to help." She smirked.

"Why don't you help a bus stop in traffic by stepping in front of it?"

"No, really, the scooter pies were a peace offering. I just wanted to show you how sorry I was that you didn't make the dance team. Guess you didn't see the note on the signup sheet, *No fat chicks*."

Her words cut deep, but Tricia tried not to show it. "Then how'd you make it? You have ten pounds of extra fat between your ears."

"A fat joke from a fat loser. How original."

"Please. We are talking," Tomoko said quietly.

Brynn shook her head. "You made the team. Why are you hanging out with this loser? I mean gainer."

"You are being unkind to my friend."

"Eat lice, Tomoko," Brynn said in an exaggerated Asian accent.

"Racist much," Tricia replied.

Brynn cackled. She pushed her eyes up at the corners. "So solly. We veddy solly you rike pig girl."

The back of Tricia's neck got hot. She clenched her fists. She had never punched another human being in her life, but Brynn hardly qualified as one so delivering her knuckles between her eyes seemed the right thing to do.

"Let's go, girls," Mustache Milton shouted, holding the locker room door open. "We have to pick teams for volleyball."

Brynn walked toward the exit. Cathi joined her. Brynn turned back to her and said, "You know, Trina, you oughta try smoking. It helps us keep trim."

"Are you kidding, Brynn?" Cathi said. "She'd have to smoke a carton a day to lose all that flab."

"Yeah, I didn't think of that. She'd die of cancer before she lost enough fat to look halfway thin."

"Do not listen to them," Tomoko said, watching the laughing girls walk out of the door. "Losing weight is not so hard."

Tricia pulled her shorts up over her thighs trying not to grunt. "What do you mean losing weight isn't so hard?"

Mustache Milton stood there with her hands on her hips. "Laps await, girls, if you don't get out there right now."

Tricia quickly tied her shoes. "You have first lunch, don't you, Tomoko? We can talk then if you want. I want to hear why you think losing weight is so easy."

"Lunch?" she replied hesitantly. "Oh, uh, yes. I was planning on going to the study hall to prepare for my history exam, but I will try to make it."

Tricia followed her out of the locker room and into the gym. She decided to put out a feeler to see if she could learn more about what she had seen that morning in Tomoko's window. "So, how do you like staying with the Henderson's? They treat you well?"

"Girls, you have five seconds to get your butts over here," Mustache Milton growled.

"We must go," Tomoko said, ignoring her question. "I do not want to run laps."

They jogged over to the volleyball court and stood with the rest of the class. Tricia had the strangest feeling that she was hiding something from her, but she had no idea what it could be.

NINE

Lunch was a power struggle between the strength of her hunger and her determination to get thin. Tricia ordered a salad and resisted the impulse to ladle on the creamy thousand island dressing. Her mom had warned her of the illusion of salads always being healthy. If you put enough of the wrong dressing on a healthy salad, it could become a calorific nightmare of fats, sugars, and oils. She settled for a red wine vinaigrette, her least favorite, and put the salad bowl on her tray. She looked for Tomoko but didn't see her. She must have gone to the study hall like she said. Tricia trudged to an empty table in the corner, set her tray down and sat in one of the curved plastic chairs. She took a bite of salad, wincing at the overdose of vinegar. Horf approached with a platter of fries, a hamburger, and a large oatmeal raisin cookie.

"Hey, Tricia." It was Horf. "Did I tell you I saw an impossibility at the zoo yesterday? An elephant with Alzheimer's."

"Have you seen Tomoko?" she asked. "She was supposed to be meeting me."

"Uh, this is where you're supposed to cough up a laugh at my keen juxtaposition of an elephant never forgetting and the ravages of dementia."

"Ha. Ha. Did you see her?"

"She was standing outside the doors like she was making up her mind to go inside. Kind of kooks. Wanna fry?"

"Of course, I want a fry, but I'm not going to have one."

"Oh, sorry. Yeah, I forgot you were going all healthy on me."

She stabbed a pink tomato chunk, dipped it in the vinaigrette, and ate it. "Yum," she said dully.

"You're really going through with this diet thing. You're not even fat."

"For a whale, I'm not. You know you could become a vegan and be my diet buddy."

"Why would I want to do that?"

"Um, because you've got a little pooch there in the belly zone."

He pinched his stomach fat between both hands. "I keep fat reserves for any starvation scenarios like war, famine, and a visit to my Aunt Lena's for glumpkes. And I'll have you know that this is a Diet Coke."

"Oh, I didn't know you had a *Diet* Coke. You'll need to tighten your belt to keep your pants from falling off."

"And rob all the girls the pleasure of seeing me in my tighty whiteys."

She laughed and took a fry, dipping it in ketchup. "One won't hurt me. I need something to remind my mouth what a tomato tastes like." She ate the hot French fry.

Horf put half his fries on a napkin and added a blob of ketchup. He pulled the tasty load next to her bowl. "Enjoy."

She clucked her tongue. "I can't eat those. They're not on my diet."

"Not true. Ketchup is made of tomatoes, right?"

"I guess."

"And tomatoes are a what?

"A vegetable."

"Technically, a fruit because they have seeds inside them, but exactly, tomatoes are a vegetable. And fries are potatoes which are a..."

46

Deadly Diet

"Starch."

"Botanically speaking, potatoes are vegetables. So, fries and ketchup have vegan up the ying-yang."

Tricia ate a wilted piece of lettuce, trying not to get a whiff of the fries. "Look, Horf, why are you undermining my diet? I do that pretty well all by myself."

"I - I'm not. I just don't think you need to lose any weight. You look great to me. I asked you out, remember?"

"Don't throw that in my face. I told you I like you as a friend. I don't want to mess that up by dating you." *Yeah, right, Tricia. You also thought he looked like the Pillsbury dough boy.*

Looking over Horf's shoulder, she spotted Tomoko stepping hesitantly into the dining hall.

She got up from the table. "I'll be right back. I have to talk to her."

She hurried toward Tomoko who looked as if she had just entered the innermost circle of Hell. She took a few steps into the lunchroom, before stopping and backing away from the kids coming off the lunch line.

"Tomoko!"

She turned away from her, slamming into the bar on the door, and bolted into the hallway.

Tricia found her sitting on the floor against the wall, shivering.

"Tomoko, what's wrong?"

She glanced over her shoulder and shuddered.

Tricia looked and saw nothing. "Are you okay?"

Tomoko propped a smile on her face. "Oh, yes. As I told you, I did not sleep well last night and am feeling anxious in my stomach."

"You look kind of pale."

"I did not eat breakfast or lunch. My stomach..."

She offered her hand to help her up. "Maybe I should take you to the clinic."

Tomoko shook her head. "I will be fine. Sometimes I feel lightheaded from my diet..."

"Wait. What diet? You look perfect. No flab or cottage cheese. You're just where I want to be."

47

Tomoko managed a weak smile. "Yes, and I wish to stay at this weight. I do not wish to go back to where I was."

"And where was that?"

Tomoko paused and then said softly, "I have lost ninety pounds."

"Ninety pounds! What? How?"

"In Japan, I loved all things American especially fast food. I gained weight—too much weight. The children at school called me *ko-ushi*, baby cow." A tear slid down her cheek at the memory.

Tricia's porky pity-party so absorbed her, she didn't even acknowledge her friend's sadness. "No, no, I mean how did you lose weight? Beverly Hills? Atkins? Fasting? I'd do anything to be as thin as you are."

"Is this true?" Tomoko said, her moist eyes suddenly alert.

"Totally. I just started doing the vegan thing this morning and I'm already sneaking junk food like crazy. What's your secret?"

The doors to the lunchroom opened and Mr. Henderson came out ambling toward them, carrying a tray of spaghetti and meatballs. The likeable big man walked duck-footed, tilting back ever so slightly as if facing a constant headwind. "Hi, Tricia. Tomoko, you have dance today, right? I'll stay in my room and grade some papers so I can give you a ride home."

Tomoko nodded but couldn't look him in the eye.

He smiled. "Come get me in my office when you're ready."

As he passed by the girls on his way to the teacher's lounge, Tomoko turned away from him, almost in a panic. "I must go."

"What's wrong?"

"I have to go to study hall. We will speak later." Tomoko flashed a smile and scuttled away in the direction of the study hall. She looked as if she were trying with all her might not to bolt full speed down the hallway.

The idea that something was wrong between Mr. Henderson and her struck Tricia as a bit more plausible than it seemed this morning. She was afraid of him. But why?

She turned to head back into the lunchroom and ran straight into another student.

"Whoa," the guy said. "Are you trying out for the football team or what?"

"Huh?" Tricia blurted. She stood face to face with Trey Curtis, the guy of her dreams. He was better looking from six inches away than the three feet that separated their desks in English class.

"You hit me like a linebacker," he said.

"Oh. Sorry, Trey."

"It's cool." He walked around her, then turned back. "I know you?"

"We have Brit Lit together."

"Mrs. Myers class? Wait. Yeah. You sit in the back row, right?"

"Yeah," she said, too embarrassed to tell him that she sat at the desk directly in front of him. "I'm Tricia. My parents went straight for the nickname."

Trey nodded. "From what?"

"Um, Patricia."

"Right. Gotcha."

For a moment, she thought that he was going to keep talking to her, but he arranged his books and continued his trip into the lunchroom.

She put on a grimace that she hoped would pass for a smile. "See you."

He didn't answer.

As she watched him walk away, her stomach sank. She sat right in front of the guy in class, and he hadn't noticed her at all. She bit her lip and vowed not to cry. And then rushed into the bathroom to break her promise.

She came out of the restroom, wiping her eyes with a tissue. Horf was standing in the hallway, pitching pennies against the wall.

"Where'd you go, Tricia?"

"Sorry. I was talking to Tomoko."

"You two smoking dope? Your eyes are all red."

"Yeah, I'm a reefer fiend. It's allergies, Horf. The pollen. You think Mr. Henderson could be abusing Tomoko?"

"What the hell? Where did that come from?"

"I don't know. I've seen her acting all nervous around him. First at his house this morning, well, I didn't see him there, but a minute ago in the hall, she ran into him and looked terrified."

"Mr. Hendo is the GOAT. We all love him. I am a hundred percent sure that he's not doing anything to Tomoko."

"It does seem kind of out there that he would do that. Still maybe I should tell somebody."

"And screw up his life by accusing him of being a child molester? There's no way he's taking advantage of her. His wife would kill him and send him straight to Hell if she found that out. And Mr. Hendo was the one who reported Coach Hale hooking up with Cassie Miles and got him prosecuted. Besides, I think Tomoko might be abusing herself."

"What do you mean?"

"Look at her. She's a fricking skeleton. I mean you can see her collarbones and her arms are sticks."

"You're exaggerating. You really have something against people who want to look their best, don't you?"

He tossed another penny. "I have something against being unhealthy for the sake of what other people think about the way I look." He offered her a toss of a coin, but I refused.

"I have to get to class, Horf. Do me a favor and don't talk to me about what I eat. Just let me do my thing."

"Just let my friend get all freaked out when she eats a Tater tot or a Snickerdoodle. Cool, that's the kind of a friend I want to be." He picked up his pennies. "How about this? What if I do your diet with you like you said?"

"What?"

"Yeah. I mean, I might make jokes about diets and stuff, but I was thinking maybe I might want to – you know—get healthier. You said yourself I'm a little heft-o."

"Wow. Just like that. One minute you say weight doesn't matter to you and then the next, you want to turn vegan. You have to do it for yourself, not because I'm struggling."

"Oh right. And you're doing it all for yourself, huh?" he said.

Deadly Diet

"You're my best friend. Going on a diet because I'm on it isn't going to change that to something more."

"I'll see you later, best friend," he said coldly. He turned away from her and marched down the hallway.

"Horf, don't be like that," she said. She ran after him and slowed him down by grabbing his arm.

He turned and faced her. Tears pooled in his eyes. "Be like what? A person who wants to help you?"

"Listen, I'm sorry," Tricia said. "You're right. You're exactly right. I'm not doing this diet for myself. I mean I am, but I'm not… Anyway, if you want to help me get through this… I mean, I really want you to help me get through this, if you're into it. What do you say?"

He wiped his eyes and said, "Pass the tofu."

She hugged him and told him she would give him the book her mom shared with her after school.

As she walked in the other direction to her next class, Tricia wondered if Horf was right about Mr. Henderson being innocent of her suspicions. She decided to feel around the edges with Tomoko and see if she could get her to open up about her relationship with her sponsor.

The rest of the day passed without incident. After the last bell rang, she found Horf at his locker and gave him her mom's book to study. He thanked her, and she hustled off to the gym to see if she could find Tomoko. She wanted to get her cell number before dance team practice so she could talk to her later.

She wasn't there. Tricia asked Mustache Milton if she had seen her, and she told her that Tomoko had gone home sick. She almost said something to the coach about what she suspected was making her sick but kept quiet. Horf was right. An unfounded accusation of child abuse against Mr. Henderson could ruin his life in a heartbeat. She would wait until she had a chance to talk to Tomoko about it before deciding what to do.

Had Tricia known at the time the truth about Tomoko Tanaka's inner demons, she would have never spoken to her again.

TEN

After Tricia got home from school and did her homework, she walked into the kitchen and opened the refrigerator as was her habit. It was time to watch her daily episode of *Buffy the Vampire Slayer* and that meant snack time for her as well. Mom had turned her onto the classic series about the undead-hunting teenager after telling her how much she and her friends had loved it when she was in college. She saw the loaf of whole wheat bread she had made the night before, sitting beside the coffee cake Dad had purchased at the bakery on his way home last night. She opened the cake box and touched the cinnamon frosting, then licked the sweet taste from her fingers. She broke off a tiny piece of cake and tasted it. Mm, so good.

She turned her attention to the loaf of bread, a certified block of bland.

She returned her interest to the sweet coffee cake. Nothing there but empty calories waiting to be converted into lumps of cottage cheese on her thighs.

Back to the bread, Tricia. Good wholesome food. Dull, but nutritious.

Deadly Diet

She grabbed the loaf and put it on the cutting board. She sliced off a thick slab and took a bite. Not as satisfying as a sugar fix, but it wasn't bad, simply different.

She chewed the bread and put the rest of the loaf back beside the coffee cake in the refrigerator. She swallowed the lump of bread and started to close the door.

The coffee cake called to her. *I'm so much tastier than that nasty, blah-blah bread. Come on, try another little piece. Or better yet, try a bigger piece and really get a taste of what you're missing.*

Her stomach answered with a gurgle.

Just one more little bite.

She opened the box and sampled another small chunk of coffee cake. She moaned with pleasure at the sweetness on her tongue.

Told you I was good. Have some more, the cake whispered.

She glanced at the slab of bread sitting on the counter, a brown brick of blech, and then focused her attention on the moist cake with the swirls of white frosting and sugar-coated walnuts. One more nibble wouldn't do any a damage. It was just a bundle of crumbs, really. As atonement, she could run an extra mile in the morning. She tore off a large hunk of coffee cake and took it with her into the living room to watch her show.

The remainder of her bread stayed on the counter until after the show, when she returned to shove it into the disposal to grind away her guilt.

ELEVEN

It was Saturday. Day seven of her weight loss plan and Tricia didn't hate waking up to run with her mom and Mrs. Alquist in the cold darkness anymore. The silence of early morning, broken only by their huffing breaths, pounding feet, and an occasional barking dog, gave her time to think about the changes that were going to happen in her life after she lost the extra weight. Boys would pay attention to her. Girls would be jealous of her dancing skills. Sure, she was having trouble staying off the junk food, but she knew if she strengthened her willpower, she would overcome. What she hated was the gurgling gassy goblin that had taken up residence in her stomach. Burps and growls during the quiet time of test taking were a sure ticket to an unwanted nickname linked to her best friend. Belch and Horf, anyone?

For the past week, she had intentionally avoided stepping on a scale, wanting to build expectation of a positive result that would propel her into the next week. Her mother claimed that she had noticed a difference in her appearance, but when she checked the mirror each day, she saw no change at all. Now, here she was standing in the bathroom about to step up and reveal the results of her efforts.

With her toe, she tapped the "on" button and the scale blinked awake, red eyes staring at her. She crossed her fingers and stepped on the metal face. The scale creaked, flashed a few times, and then revealed her weight.

One-forty-four.

She had lost one pound!

She stared at the disappointing result, biting her lip. One fricking pound for a whole week of suffering! All that early morning pavement pounding, all those daily battles with hunger, all those afternoons of skipping snacks or eating bland ones, all that effort to lose one lousy, measly pound.

She stepped off the scale and then stepped on again to make sure that it had been working properly. The results were the same. One-forty-four. One puny fricking pound. Her fingers curled into fists.

Her mother stuck her head into the bathroom. "Well?"

Tricia stepped off the scale and turned to her. "Some great diet, Mom. It's a loser except when it comes to losing weight, just like your daughter."

"What do you mean?"

"One fricking pound. I ate all your stupid salads, enough stupid vegetables to grow rabbit ears and enough brown rice to feed an army of those Hare Krishna dudes at the park and I lost one fricking pound."

"And you didn't have any snacks in between?"

"Not really," she said, excluding a few smuggled candy bars from Penny's room, a handful of brownies from the school cafeteria, a couple of potato chips that turned into a whole bag, a slice or two of coffee cake, whatever. "I should have lost four or five pounds easy, not one stupid, waste-of-time, put-it-back-in-an-hour pound."

She put her hand on her daughter's shoulder. "That's how you're supposed to lose weight, honey. You didn't put all those extra pounds on in a week, did you?"

Tricia stared at the scale. "At this rate, it'll be months before I get to where I want to be, maybe years."

"Stop being a drama queen. You're doing great."

Penny and her Suzy Chatterbox doll skipped into the bathroom. She sank her teeth into a chewy granola bar that wouldn't add an ounce of fat to her. Sometimes, Tricia hated her.

"Whatcha all doing?" Penny asked, taking another bite of the bar.

"Talking," Mom said.

"'Bout what?"

"None of your business," Tricia snapped.

Mom huffed. "Just because you didn't lose what you thought you should is no reason to be mean to your sister."

Penny took a third big bite of the bar. Tricia was counting.

"Trichtcha Wicha, ooh wanson?" Translation from chewy granola speak: "Tricia, you want some?"

"No."

"Why? Cause you're so fat? That's what you always say. You don't want any 'cause you're so fat!"

"Make like a ghost and vanish, you little turdpile," Tricia said.

"Please stop calling her that," Mom said.

"I don't think you're so fat," Penny said. "And Suzy doesn't think you're so fat, do you, Suzy?" She squeezed the doll's middle finger.

"No, Momsuds," Suzy said.

"Will you and that dumb doll get the heck out of here?" Tricia said. "You're such a fricking pest."

"Language, Tricia. You know I don't like that word fricking."

"Yeah, fatty patty yam butt," Penny said. "Mom doesn't like your cursing."

"Buzz off before I pull your doll's head off."

Penny clutched Suzy to her chest. "Momsuds!"

Mom sighed. "Tricia, come on. Penny, why don't you go see what your dad is up to in his workshop?"

"Let's go, Suzy," Penny huffed. She ate the last of the oats and chocolate, and left the room, holding the doll in tow by the hand.

Tricia folded her arms and said, "I'm going on that carnivore diet. I read that you can lose ten pounds in ten days on it. Ten pounds in ten days sounds a lot better than ten pounds in ten weeks. And I can get one of those rubber sweatsuits to run in, so I lose weight even faster. Two weeks of suffering, max, and then I start eating normally again."

"Not happening, Tricia. The carnivore diet is a fad with mixed scientific evidence. As far as wearing a rubber sweat suit, in a word, not a chance in the world."

"I'm sixteen. I should be able to do what I want."

"I'm forty and I can't do what I want. Trust me, just stick with what you're doing, and you'll get to where you want to be."

Tricia snicked her tongue against her teeth and pushed past her. "I have to get ready. Horf and I are going skating. I'll just have toast for breakfast."

"With some fruit and you'll have to make it yourself. Oh, and you can't go skating until later."

"What?"

"I'm going to the co-op, remember? I volunteered to work there this morning in exchange for shopping chits."

"Oh yeah, you told me that."

"I won't be gone all day so you can still go skating. You'll have to babysit Penny until I get back. Hopefully, you'll be in a better mood." She kissed her on the cheek and left her standing in the bathroom.

Tricia dressed and stomped downstairs into the kitchen. She cut a slice of whole wheat bread from the loaf and dropped it into the toaster. She glanced at her distorted reflection in the steel appliance. The Blimp Woman from Fat City.

Her phone buzzed in her pocket. It was a text from Horf. *Are we still going?*

She texted: *Have to go later. Babysitting. Wanna hang 'til then?*
CU in a few.

The toast popped.

She put her phone into her pocket. She opened the fridge to get the plant butter with olive oil. She ignored the slice of birthday cake from the party Penny had attended yesterday. She grabbed the tub of fake butter and smeared ample amounts of it on her slice of toast. She wolfed it down with a glass of almond milk and then grabbed a banana.

There was a knock at the entryway.

Penny ran to the foyer and opened the door. She yelled, "Trisha Wisha, It's your boyyyyfriend."

Tricia winced and poked her head out of the kitchen. Horf slouched into the house, pulling the hoodie off his head. He smoothed his hand over his mussed hair, but it was more of a habit than an improvement. His bright eyes belied his attempts at casual indifference.

"I'm in here," she called.

Horf rambled into the kitchen where she was putting dishes in the dishwasher. They exchanged heys. Penny followed.

"Banana?" Tricia asked him.

"Just ate."

"Whatcha doing today, Horf? You and Trisha Wisha gonna play kissy face?" Penny giggled.

Tricia shook her head. "No, we're going to play hide and seek. You go hide and we'll come find you."

"Nuh uh. Last time I played with you, you didn't even look for me. I hid under the bed for a half hour."

"Then go watch your shows or play with Suzy, whatever."

"So, you two can play kissy face." She made smooching sounds.

"You want me to call Mom and tell her that you're not doing what I say."

Penny grabbed a couple of cookies from the pantry. "Smooch. Smooch." She giggled and ran into the family room.

"Why does she always call me your boyfriend?" Horf asked. "You change your mind about me?"

"Horf…"

"I'm kidding, I'm kidding."

"Who knows why she does anything? Why does she eat a gazillion calories a day and never gain a pound? I look at a piece of cake and gain two. She's just obnoxious."

"I don't see what the prob is," he said. "I mean, just quit eating all that sweet stuff and stick to the health plan."

"It's not that easy, Horf."

"I'm doing it. Just say no to blub."

"You wouldn't think it was funny if you were fat."

"In case you forgot, I am fat, but I don't worry about it like you do. I'm sticking to the plan and so far, I've lost four pounds." He pinched his fat and shook it.

"What? Four freaking pounds!" Tricia cried, accidentally squeezing her banana to mush. "I lost one. How the hell? That's it. I'm going to start eating just meat. If I limit myself to one kind of food, it will be easier to stick to it."

"No, it won't. It's just gonna make you feel bad and make it way harder to stay away from the sweets."

"Listen to this guy, Dr. Diet Expert. A week ago, you were wolfing down pizza, hot dogs, and chocolate pudding."

"But not all at the same time, Dominoes doesn't have hot-dog-pudding-pizza-pie on the menu yet."

"Doing it right takes too long. I don't care what you or my mom says, I'm going carnivore."

"And how are you going to stop using food as Xanax when you're feeling stressed out?"

"Wow. All of sudden, you're also an expert on emotional eating. Hey, I have an idea, Dr. Horf, why don't you just prescribe me some appetite suppressants to keep my hunger away."

"Now you're thinking straight," he said mockingly.

She poured a plastic cup of water and offered it to him. He thanked her and took a sip. she poured herself a drink as well and gulped half of it.

"Actually, that's a boss idea," she said. "But how can I get diet pills without a doctor's prescription?"

Horf coughed a laugh. "Are you for real? Diet pills will make you all anxious and twitchy. Wait, forget anxious and twitchy. What would your parents do if they found out you were popping diet pills?"

"Restriction for life? Toss my cell phone into the Columbia River and give me a tin can and a string? What I need is a non-prescription miracle pill with no side effects except massive weight loss. You know where I can get one of those?"

Vincent Courtney

"Sure, only it's the size of a basketball. Seriously, Tricia, you can do this. I'll be there for you, whenever you want me to be," Horf said softly, putting his hand on her shoulder.

"You can help me more if you stop trying to use a diet to get together with me."

His face fell and she immediately regretted her snippy but accurate comment. "Sorry."

"Screw you," he snapped. "It's not my fault you can't keep your mouth closed, and I don't mean shoving cookies into it. I'm trying to be your friend here."

Her hackles rose. "Sure, you are. A friend with benefits."

He slammed the cup of water on the counter. "I'm out of here, Tricia. You're just pissing me off now."

"Okay, 'bye."

Tricia opened the kitchen door for him. He stepped past without looking at her. She slammed the door harder than she should have. Mad at Horf for losing four times as much weight as her and pretending he wasn't still trying to date her. Mad at herself for arguing against losing weight in a sensible way. Mad about the whole stupid mess.

She grabbed her glass of water and stomped out of the kitchen. She joined Penny in the family room where she was watching some dumb kid's show about Morris the Talking Moose.

"Where's your boyfriend, Trisha Wisha?"

"He had to go home and stop calling him my boyfriend."

"You don't like him?"

"Of course, I like him a lot, just not as a boyfriend."

"How come?"

Tricia drank the rest of her water. "I can't talk to you."

She stomped back into the kitchen to refill her glass. Her anger morphed slowly into guilt, her constant companion since starting this diet crap. Here Horf was making sense about losing weight in a reasonable way, and she had hammered the stuffing out of him.

She dialed his number. He didn't answer. She texted him an apology, waited just long enough to realize he wasn't going to reply, before tucking her phone into her back pocket. She wanted to pull her hair out. Such a witch. Such a stupid, stupid witch. She had just cost herself the one good friend that she had at Bitterbrook High.

She texted Mandy and Megan to air her confession and seek solace in their advice on what she should do to fix her relationship with Horf, but neither responded. That meant both were either still asleep after staying out late Friday night or dead, those being the only possible explanations as to why they would be without their phones. She would have to wait for one of them to wake up before she heard back.

Hurt and frustrated, Tricia reflexively opened the fridge to see what might be in there to lower her stress level from total panic to slight worry. She saw her medication sitting under a layer of transparent plastic wrap pulled taut over the plate that held it.

"Happy birthday to me," she whispered.

TWELVE

As Tricia lay in her bed, an unpleasant heaviness churning in her stomach crushed the momentary surge of pleasure that she had received from inhaling the sugary slab of cake. She closed her eyes and willed her gut back to normal. It didn't last. Something thick and oily roosted in her throat. She swallowed hard to make it go away. Her stomach lurched and a splash of bitter acid burned her esophagus.

Her phone buzzed. It was Mandy.

"First thing, Tee. It's an unwritten law of the sexes," she said. "Guys do not make good best friends. They always fall in love with you."

"Don't agree. Once Horf gets a girlfriend, we'll be cool. If I didn't mess up our friendship big time by being such a tool. It's just that this diet is making me depressed and as hangry as a pissed off pig. One pound I lost. A week of trying and I lost one fricking pound. So, what do I do? I gorph down a giant slice of birthday cake because I messed up my relationship with my best friend. Ugh."

The thick oily thing clambered into her throat again. Her mouth filled with saliva. She gulped once, twice.

"The guy likes you, right?" Mandy asked. "Dating-likes."

"I guess. It was my dig about him wanting more from our relationship than friendship that pissed him off and made him leave." Her throat felt full. She swallowed.

"Then all you have to do is apologize. If he feels that way about you, he'll cave."

"You can be evil. You know that."

"And right, too."

The thing climbed onto the back of her tongue. She burped a bubble of acid.

"What was that?" Mandy asked. "Sounded like a toad."

Her stomach started to hurt. "Uh oh."

"What?"

Tricia sat up in bed and took a deep breath, trying to stave off the approaching sickness.

"Tee?"

"I'm gonna have to get off. I don't feel right. Later, Mando."

The juggernaut of regurgitation had started and there was nothing she could do to stop it. She jumped up from the bed and barely made it to the bathroom before the birthday cake made a second and decidedly less appealing appearance.

After she finished, she flushed away her shame. She wiped her face with a cool wet cloth and brushed her teeth. She staggered back into the bedroom and lay on the bed. The whole episode revolted her. How could anyone voluntarily stick their fingers down their throats and do the binge-purge thing every day?

"You all right, Trisha Wisha?" Penny asked, poking her head into her room. "I heard you puking."

"I ate something that made me sick, but I'm fine now. Don't tell Mom, okay? I don't want her to think I have the flu or something."

"Kay. Can I have that piece of birthday cake from Sierra's party?"

"Um, I was making room in the fridge, and I accidentally dropped it on the floor."

"You throwed it away?"

"Sorry. I don't think Mom would want me serving you cake that I scraped off the kitchen floor."

"Your phone's buzzing."

Tricia looked at the screen to see if it might be Horf or Megan. It was a number she didn't recognize. She sat up in bed. The foul taste in her mouth reminded her of the cake purge. "Privacy."

"What's Mom's magic message?" Penny asked.

"Privacy, please," she said, then added, "Before I lock you in the closet."

Penny giggled and ran into the other room. Tricia put the phone to her ear.

"Is this Tricia Hall from Bitterbrook High?" a fast-talking girl said.

"Yes?"

"Tricia Hall from Bitterbrook High, you have been selected as a contestant on our new YouTube Channel, *Useless Facts You Never Thought You'd Use.*"

"Huh?"

"It's our trivia contest. If you win, you get a free dinner for two from our sponsor Fatburgers. Now, here are your three questions."

"Who is this?"

"Number one. What is the biggest animal on the face of the earth?"

"Who are you again?"

"Five seconds."

"Is this for real?"

"Four… three … two …"

"A blue whale," Tricia blurted, suspicious, but not wanting to hang up on the off chance that the call might be for real.

"That's right. Question number two. What animal is known as the river horse?" I heard laughter on the other end of the line.

"This is a joke."

"A hippo. That's right. And number three, what do both of these animals have in common? That's right. They're both super fat and they can both dance better than you."

The caller hung up amid uproarious laughter.

"Stupid bitch Brynn," she hissed, hanging up. Mom must have given her cell number to Mrs. Alquist, and she must have given it to

Deadly Diet

Brynn believing that she could help along a friendship. Mrs. Alquist must also believe the Tooth Fairy and Santa Claus had an affair at Bigfoot's house.

Penny skipped into the room. "Who was it?"

"Wrong number," she said.

"What's a matter?" Penny asked.

"Just leave me alone, Penny, okay?"

"Why are you all sad faced," Penny said. She scuffed her feet, shuffling toward the door. "I don't like seeing you that way."

She pressed her palms into her eyes and wiped them. She smiled at her little sister. "It's nothing. I just let some stupid girls get to me for a minute. It won't happen again." She took a deep breath and said, "Come here, you little turdpile."

Penny grinned with relief and ran over to give her a big hug. Her eyes brightened. "You wanna play some house? I'll be the mommy and you and Suzy can be my kids."

"As long as you're not serving cake," she replied.

Her phone buzzed again. She didn't recognize the number but had a feeling Brynn and Cathi had not finished messing with her.

She answered it. "Listen, you two haters..."

"Tricia, it is Tomoko. I am sorry I did not see you at school. I have been... sick but am better now." Her sunny tone of voice seemed forced. "I need to talk to you."

"To me?"

"Can you come to the Henderson home tonight? I will be alone then."

"Alone? Is anything wrong?"

"No. Nothing. Please come."

"You're not going to tell me what it's about?"

Tomoko had hung up the phone, leaving her unsettled about the nature of her call.

THIRTEEN

Bitterbrook was a creepy place at night, especially out on Thirteen Corners Road, where the shifting shadows of the woods clawed at your commonsense, conjuring spirits of the forest and lurking beasts. The pounding rain added to her apprehension about driving on the deserted snaking road. Tricia didn't want to hydroplane on the wet surface of the pavement to end up careening down the steep embankment into the trunk of a Douglas fir.

The threat of losing control of her mom's Camry was not her only concern about driving to the Henderson's. For most of the afternoon, she had been thinking about the strange urgency of Tomoko's call. Was it possible that the beloved Mr. Hendo was actually a soon-to-be-hated Mr. Pedo? Was she walking into what could be a dangerous situation should Mr. Henderson come home at the wrong time? It was time to call in reinforcements. She told Siri to call Horf hoping he would answer his phone this time.

He did.

"Don't kill me," she blurted. "I phone in peace."

Deadly Diet

"Oh, hi, Tricia," he said, his tone cool. "What's up?"

"First off, I'm super sorry about being such a major B earlier. I wish I could shove it all back into my big mouth like I do a handful of cookies, but I can't, so an apology is all I've got."

"That's okay. I'm over it."

"It's not okay. You're my best bud, and I shouldn't go off like that."

"Maybe I am turning into a bit of a nutri-nerd. At the moment, I'm obsessed with eating the right things."

"Look, you found something that works for you, and you want it to work for me. I appreciate that, but I didn't just call to apologize."

"What's going on?"

"Tomoko called me this morning, acting all nice, but kind of sketchy."

"What do you mean?"

"She needed to talk to me she said. Alone. She even made a point of telling me that the Henderson weren't going to be there. You don't think she wants to tell me about, you know, Mr. Henderson touching her inappropriately."

"I'm telling you that Mr. Hendo wouldn't do that. You're letting your imagination go a little kooks."

"You're right. I'm on my way over there right now. I could pick you up."

"I'm at work. Old Man Grunion ordered an all-hands special inventory because he thinks everybody's ripping him off."

"That sucks. You can't take an hour off?"

"No. I'm just a menial cog in the corporate machine. Besides, I'm getting paid overtime."

"Well, enjoy counting cans while I accuse everybody's favorite teacher of being a pedophile."

"Don't be like that. I'm telling you you're way off. Call me once you find out what the Japanese toothpick tells you."

"I'll let you know." I hung up.

Streetlights traced white lines of rain down to the shining street where the Henderson's lived. The houses were an assortment of bungalows, foursquares, and ranch style homes, none were huge but

67

all comfortable. Tricia parked in the driveway, climbed out of the car, and walked up the sidewalk. The knot in her stomach was a half-hitch wrapped around a sheepshank. She knocked the snow off her shoes before stepping onto the porch and ringing the doorbell.

Holly Henderson surprised her when she answered the door. She was a tall girl made taller by a stack of curly red hair. She pushed a bubble of gum back into her mouth. "Are you looking for Tomoko?"

"We're supposed to hang out."

She nodded. "Come in."

Tricia stepped into the house and walked into the living room that put out major logging vibes. Hanging above the worn leather couch was a folk-art painting of a Portland lumber operation manned by bearded men with heads too big for their bodies covered in red flannel shirts with pants tucked into boots. Forest creatures made unintentionally giant by the artist's lack of skill regarding perspective watched from the nearby woods. A three-foot high statue of Paul Bunyan stood next to the woodbin beside the fireplace, his blue ox Babe stood on the other side.

"Was one of your relatives a lumberjack?" Tricia asked with a smile.

"Not that I know of. Why?"

"Uh, the painting, Paul Bunyan."

"Oh," she said. "That junk came with the rental."

She popped her gum and called upstairs, "Tricia's here."

Tomoko appeared at the top of the stairs. She looked thinner than the last time she had seen her a week ago, almost gaunt. She must have had a stomach bug. Tricia wondered if she could catch it from her and lose a few pounds that way herself. Sick, right?

She motioned for her to follow her up the stairs and into her room.

Tricia didn't know why, but she expected to see black ink paintings of tiny birds sitting on bamboo limbs and to smell incense burning inside a brass pot decorated with dragons. Instead, she saw posters of Dayglo, the boy band of the moment, a laptop sitting on a mahogany desk, and a poster bed with a pink quilt covering it. She spotted only one reminder of Tomoko's homeland sitting on the dresser in her room. It was an exquisitely detailed keepsake box with tassel pulls to open it.

Deadly Diet

"That's pretty. What's in there?"

She opened the box and showed Tricia her collection. "This is my ticket stub for the concert of Lady Gaga." She picked up a small smoking pipe and sniffed it. "This is the *kiseru* of my grandfather. I keep it because the smell of the tobacco reminds me of him." She put it back and handed her what looked to be a luggage tag made of red silk with detailed embroidery.

"What's this?"

"And this is *omamori*, an amulet from the Shinto shrine. It brings good fortune."

"Like a rabbit's foot only not cruel and barbaric. Awesome."

She smiled.

"So, uh, what did you want to talk about, Tomoko?" *Please don't let it be what I think it is. Please, please, please.*

She kept the smile, but it didn't light her eyes. "Do you still want to lose weight?"

"What?" Tricia said. It sounded more like a huff of relief than the actual word.

"You want to lose weight, is this not so?"

"Yes, of course, I want to lose weight. Is that what you wanted to talk to me about? I mean the way you were being so mysterious on the phone. I thought..." She laughed. "You don't want to know what I thought."

Tomoko walked over to her dresser and pulled out a small pouch. It looked like the bag that contained the magic beans in *Jack and the Beanstalk*. She shook a few pills out into her hand. They were light brown with darker brown speckles.

"These will make you lose weight."

"What are they?"

"They are called *Hangakira*."

"*Hangakira*?"

"It is Japanese meaning 'hunger killer.'"

"And those are what made you lose all that weight?"

"Oh, yes," she said. "Take one pill in the morning and you will not eat all day."

"Are they, you know, legal? Never mind, I don't want to know." I took one of the pills and examined it. "How did you find out about these?"

Tomoko continued. "When I weighed so much, I went on diet after diet, losing weight, then gaining it back. My failure would trigger eating binges to punish myself."

Tricia felt her pain, having known it intimately herself.

Tomoko continued. "I was so desperate I stole a valuable ring of my mother's so that I could pay for a weight loss retreat in the mountains. I told mother and father that I had won the trip in a contest, and they let me go. When I arrived at the retreat, I met a girl there and she told me about the pills."

"What's in them?"

"I do not know. Herbs, powders. I only know that they work to make it easy to stop eating."

"Ancient Asian Dexatrim. I like it."

Tomoko gasped at something behind Tricia.

She turned to look but saw nothing. "What?"

The Japanese girl smiled with embarrassment. "I saw a *gokiburi* crawling down the wall, a cockroach, but it went behind the trashcan." She shuddered. "I have an unnecessary fear of them."

"Me, too. Roaches freaked me out so bad in Florida that when we moved, I googled *roach infestations* and *Portland* and got an article that said the native species sticks to the woods, so they have no issues."

"I believe the invasive species sometimes comes in produce."

"How did we get off on this? We were talking about your diet pills. How much do you want?"

Tomoko's eyes widened. She turned away from her, hesitated for a moment, and then said, "I cannot. I – I cannot."

"Come on. How much?"

"No, I cannot do this. I am sorry…" She peered over her shoulder again. A cold look of fear froze her face. I thought she was going to scream.

"What is it, Tomoko? What's the matter with you?"

"*Gokiburi. Gokiburi.*"

"Where?" Tricia turned but saw no insects.

Deadly Diet

Tomoko realized what she had said. She took a deep breath and said, "Forgive me."

"Do you want to go downstairs to get away from the roach?"

"No. It is gone now."

Tricia got back to the matter at hand. "So how much for the pills?"

"I want nothing for the pills. I will give them to you, but..."

"Is there something you're not telling me?"

She nodded. "There is something important that you must do before the pills will work."

"What's that?"

"You will find it strange," Tomoko said.

"Tell me what it is, and I'll tell you if I find it strange," she said impatiently.

"You must first read the invocation," she said. "It is most important."

She heard the soft rustle of the curtains. "What was that?"

"The Henderson's cat."

The heater kicked on and a warm gust of air brushed past her hair.

"What's the purpose of this invocation? What am I invoking?"

"I know it will sound silly to you, but it is what the girl told me to do. You are summoning *Hangakira* the spirit warrior that will give you the will to control your appetite. *Anata wa tabemasen.* You will not eat."

"I thought the pills were called *hangakira*."

"The pills and the spirit are one."

Tomoko shifted and looked unsettled. She reached into the bag and removed a small scroll made of parchment. "Now we will begin." She unrolled the parchment and handed it to her. Underneath the Japanese characters, someone had written in brown ink the English phonetic translation of the summoning. "Speak the words exactly as written."

Tricia turned when she thought she heard someone coming down the hallway.

"It's the cat," Tomoko said quickly. "She is always in the hallway. Now, you must say the invocation."

"I feel kind of dopey."

"Do you wish to lose the weight or not?"

71

She nodded and silently read the words to familiarize herself with them, even though she had no idea what the heck she was saying. It could have been a grocery list for all she knew, and Tomoko was sharing a private laugh with herself at her expense.

Tomoko closed her eyes and said with a slight tremor in her voice, "You must say it now."

Tricia shrugged and slowly read the strange words aloud. She became aware of a cold draft slipping down the back of her neck. She finished the invocation with a phrase that sounded like *Tah-kay-da Ayumee Heemay, wata-seen-OH tom-ah-see-wah nah-tah-no-mon-oh-dess.*

Tomoko groaned and sagged. She opened her eyes. For a moment, just a split second, Tricia thought she saw Tomoko's shadow move in a different direction away from her body. The Japanese girl giggled.

"What's so funny?" Tricia asked.

She handed her the pouch of pills. "I express my joy… for you. It is yours now. All yours. I have lost enough."

Tricia put the pouch in her purse, and Tomoko giggled again. It was awkward, not a joyful sound, but one of relief. They tried to talk afterwards, but found they had nothing else to say to each other, so Tricia left and walked in the drizzle to her mom's car.

On the way home, she began to consider what she had done, and she giggled, too. It had become so important for her to lose weight that she'd resorted to saying a load of hoodoo woo-woo over a bag of diet pills. The things people do in the name of ego.

She patted the pouch of pills on the other seat, her keys to success, and smiled. Out of the corner of her eye, she caught something moving in the back seat. She glanced in the rearview mirror but saw nothing there. Must have been the shifting shadows caused by the lights of a passing car.

But what if it wasn't a passing shadow? What if she had left the car door unlocked when she went inside the Henderson's? What if someone had slipped into the back seat while she was there—a pervert or a killer?

She glanced in the rearview mirror again. A pair of hateful eyes were glaring at her. She gasped, snuck the canister of pepper spray her mom insisted she carry from her purse, and turned around ready to blast the creep in the eyes. She saw the back seat and nothing more.

The car lurched into the other lane. She spun around, dropped the can, and grabbed the wheel to return to the correct one. Her sweaty palms gripped the rigid plastic. She wiped her hands on her jeans and clutched the steering wheel again. She was sweating from the doubled-up jolt of fear. For a moment, she thought she was going to be sick, but the nausea settled into a dull ache. The twin shots of adrenaline left her feeling clammy and anxious. She turned the radio up louder, but the noise only jangled her nerves further. She turned it off, but the silence was worse, dead air on which all fearful demons could dance around her. She glanced in the rearview mirror and saw two glowing eyes coming toward her again. She screamed before she realized the eyes were the headlights of a car coming around a bend in the road behind her. Was that what she had seen before, a car peeking around a corner before disappearing?

Unnerved, Tricia drove the rest of the way home as fast as she could. When she got out of the car, she heard a thin peal of laughter behind her. It sounded both faint and close at the same time. She didn't bother to turn around. She ran into the house and locked the door behind her. It was then she realized that the harrowing trip home had rattled her so much that she had left the pouch of pills on the front seat of the car.

For a moment, she considered waiting until morning to get it, but decided that she was being silly. There was no one out there. The creepy woods lining Thirteen Corners Road had played with her mind, making her see things that weren't there. She turned on the outside light and grabbed the cannister of pepper spray from her purse, just in case, and scurried outside to grab the pills.

FOURTEEN

The smell of bacon grabbed Tricia by the nose and pulled her away from her desk where she had just finished proofreading her essay about global warming. Her stomach rumbled. After she and her mother got home from their run, Dad must have pretty- pleased Mom into cooking his favorite breakfast food, despite its top standing on her list of most reviled meat products, "Nothing but nitrites and fat." Dad could be pretty persuasive when it came to his love of the salty, sweet pork-belly. In fact, he loved it so much, pigs hired hitmen to rub him out. Bacon also meant Mom made buttermilk pancakes since Dad, Penny and Tricia always made sandwiches out of them stuffed with bacon and lots of syrup. She'd wait until lunch to start on her latest diet plan. One last fling with flavor.

No.

I won't do it.

She walked to her dresser and tugged open the drawstrings of the pouch containing the keys to her success. She removed one of the speckled pills. She licked it and tasted a slightly bitter flavor. Hickory-smoked bacon and a syrup-soaked pancake would get rid of that taste in one sweet bite.

"Stop. I'm not going to give in," she said aloud as if the sound of her voice would solidify her will. She thought of Tomoko and her slim, admirable figure. *She was perfect. Perfect, like I'm going to be.* What was it that she said about the pills? *'Anata wa tabemasen.'* You will not eat.

Tricia marched into the bathroom and popped the pill, washing it down with a handful of water. She waited. She didn't know what she expected to feel, some kind of mystical healing warmth or a sudden craving for celery and grapefruit.

She felt nothing.

"Tricia, come on, breakfast is ready," Mom called from downstairs.

"Be there in a sec," she replied. She waited for some kind of sign that the pills were working but felt no indication of their effectiveness.

As she bounded down the stairs, a wicked chill passed through her as if walking through a column of unnatural chilly air rising from the middle of the stairs. She stopped and shivered. She passed her hand through the air behind her, but the space was as warm as the rest of the house. She shrugged off the chill as a side effect of the pill.

Abruptly, visions flashed inside her head: a room with wood floors and sliding paper-panel doors. Women dressed in kimonos bathed her in hot water. A whip struck one of the girls on the back. Her lips turned up in a smile. And then the disturbing visions were gone.

The sudden hallucinations were worrisome. The pills may have something in them she hadn't counted on. Oh, well, Tomoko seemed to have been able to deal with them and lose weight, and so would she.

As she approached the dining room, she noticed an unpleasant smoky odor had overpowered the savory sweet smell of the bacon. Now, she didn't want to accuse Mom of burning the bacon on purpose, but Mom had burned the bacon on purpose. She detested the fatty, salty pork belly and didn't want to pollute her family by serving it.

But what if Tricia was unjustly accusing her mother of second-degree arson of an unsuspecting pig part? There was another possibility. What if this was how the pills worked? What if the *Hangakira* spirit warrior possessed Mom and made her burn our food?

It could be. Possession is nine points of the law of Asian diet remedies. She smiled. Horf's whack sense of humor must be rubbing off on her.

She joined her family. Dad was sitting at the dining room table and reading the news on his phone. Penny was spoon-feeding air to her Suzy Chatterbox doll. Mom walked into the dining room carrying two plates, one loaded with bacon and the other stacked with pancakes.

"Against my better judgment," she said setting the plate of bacon on the table. "Just two slices, Penny."

Her sister nodded and took four. Mom put two of them back.

"Burn the first batch of bacon, Mom?" Tricia asked with a smile.

"What?"

"That burnt smell." She gestured toward the air around them.

"Burnt smell?"

"You don't smell that?"

"No, I don't, and I didn't burn anything in the kitchen. You smell anything smoky, Alan?"

Dad sniffed the air. "Nope. Did you smell it upstairs?"

"On the way downstairs."

"Hmmm, I better go check," Dad said, getting up from the table. "Might be a short in the wiring."

"I'll check down here," Mom replied.

Dad nodded and sniffed his way up the stairs.

Mom turned back to Penny and her. "You two eat your breakfast before it gets cold."

Tricia stabbed her one-pancake breakfast and put it on her plate where it lay like a slab of flayed skin. The smoky reek hit her square in her nose. It now smelled more like burnt plastic. Really foul. "Come on. You don't smell that?"

Penny folded her pancake over the two slices of bacon. "Smell what?"

"That burnt smell."

"I don't smell anything. Do you, Suzy?"

She grabbed the back of the doll's head and turned it from side to side.

Tricia sniffed her clothes. Nothing but the clean scent of fresh laundry. She took a whiff of her pancake. The burnt plastic stink was so strong that she felt woozy. She held the plate in front of Penny. "You really can't smell that?"

Penny shrugged and took a bite from her bacon pancake sandwich.

Her parents came back into the dining room. Dad sat at his place at the table and said, "The window in your room was open just a crack. Mr. Cranston must be burning leaves again."

"That was what you smelled," Mom added.

"But …"

Tricia stopped.

It hit her.

The pill.

She had taken the pill, and all of a sudden, she was smelling burnt plastic, and unable to eat. *Hangakira*, hunger killer; the name said it all. Something in the pills, an ancient herb or a powder made from goat horns or something, altered her sense of smell and in that way, murdered her appetite. Wow, this was going to be so easy.

And suck so bad.

"Now, that the mystery of the burning brush has been laid to rest, I'm going to enjoy my bacon," Dad said, slapping a handful of slices onto the pancake on his plate. "And enjoy reading the news." He folded it and took an unhealthy bite of goodness. Mom shook her head.

Tricia smiled and got up from the table.

"Are you done already?" Mom asked.

"I ate a couple of pancakes while you guys were sniffing out the smell," she said. She glanced at Penny to see if she'd report the deception, but she was too busy stuffing her face to notice. Of course, she made no mention of the pills because her mother would take them away from her in a heartbeat. Drugs, natural or artificial, were at the very top of her mother's taboo list.

"Next time, don't eat so fast," she said. "It's not good for the digestion."

She nodded and pounded upstairs to get ready for school.

When the bus arrived at Bitterbrook High, Tricia bounded off the steps and landed in a puddle that almost made her ditch. Her stomach rumbled again, a tiger on the prowl. She wondered why her appetite had returned so quickly. One pill didn't last as long as Tomoko said it would. She zipped her Orlando Magic windbreaker and followed her fellow zombies toward the entrance to the school. She sniffed the air, but there was no trace of the caustic odor of smoke.

"So, why didn't you call me last night?" Horf said from behind her. She turned and waited for him. He wore a lightweight hoodie and black pants with his belt cinched enough to put wrinkles in the waistband.

"Don't you ever wear a jacket, Horf?"

"Why? It's warm inside so I have to keep taking it on and off, putting it on the back of my chair. I figure I'll just be cold for a little while and save myself the hassle."

"Good plan," she said. "As in dumb plan."

Horf popped a sugar free mint into his mouth and offered one to her. She took it and dropped it onto her tongue, hoping it would taste right. It was fine.

"What did Tomoko have to say last night?" Horf asked.

She didn't want to get into taking the pills that made things smell bad and get an earful of "What? Are you fricking kooks?" She shrugged. "She had some ideas about how I could make my diet work for me. Then we just hung out, talked about school and what Japan is like, girl stuff. How was work?"

"How fun could it be? I spent the night counting cans and listening to Bone Fenimore tell me about his new girlfriend. Jeez, you'd think that the guy had never kissed a girl before. Can we get inside? I'm freezing my buns off."

The bell rang for first period.

As they hustled through the school's main entrance, they hit the smell of spaghetti sauce coming from the cafeteria. Before the door shut, a last gasp of cold hit the back of Tricia's neck and made her shiver. A vision flashed in her mind. It was a samurai sitting in front of her, dragging a knife across his bared mid-section. A thrill of pleasure cut through her. She slammed into Horf who had stopped at his locker.

"Tricia, watch where you're going," Horf said. "You're going to give me whiplash."

Deadly Diet

The collision snapped her out of this unsettling vision. Those pills were really messing with her head. It was then she noticed that underneath the aroma of garlic and tomato sauce was an acrid stench like burning tires.

"Man, what is that smell?" Horf asked, wrinkling his nose.

"You smell it? Like burnt rubber."

"Burnt rubber? It smells like a rank fart." He looked around them. "There it is." He pointed to a dog turd sitting on top of the trash can.

"Oh, sick!" She held her breath. "Who put that there? Somebody needs to call the janitor."

They hurried past the stinking prank. When Tricia was able to breathe again without fear of gagging, she took a deep, warm breath of air. The stench of dog droppings and burnt tires was gone.

When they reached his classroom, she and Horf parted company. She would see him in class during the following two periods and then finish her day with him in the last two classes.

She hustled to Mr. Applebee's class where she would hear a lot of bad jokes and a little bit of history. As he began class with a lame joke involving a horse, a pig and a camel, the tiger of hunger inside her began to prowl again. It paused to sharpen its claws on her stomach wall. She tried to ignore it, but it was relentless. She needed to ask Tomoko why she was still having such nagging hunger pangs after taking the pill.

For the next two classes, Tricia inflicted growls and gurgles upon her classmates. Listening to her stomach's impromptu gassy performance, Horf got the giggles in the middle of chemistry class and the teacher sent him outside until he was able to control himself.

Finally, fourth-period gym class rolled around. She hurried into the locker room to find Tomoko for a quick tutorial on how she overcame the hunger she felt. The smell of chlorine, stale towels, scented soap, and a myriad of perfumes assaulted her. She took a moment to absorb the punishment from the mingled odors before wading into the locker room to find Tomoko. She didn't see her among the girls dressing for class. She walked into the gym to see if she was there. She wasn't.

Tricia returned to her locker to get ready for class. She squeezed into her gym clothes, still keeping an eye out for Tomoko. No luck. She pulled the waistband of her shorts as far as it would stretch, hoping to break the elastic a little and loosen its hold on her belly.

Brynn came around the corner and leaned against the locker next to mine. She pulled a sweet-smelling stick of Juicy Fruit gum from the pack in her hand and added it to the huge wad of gum in her mouth. "Hey, Trina, shorts a little tight? Better buy a bigger size next time."

A chill cut through Tricia. She knew what was coming. She turned away from Brynn to avoid the smell of the gum and the stink it would bring. "Buzz off, I'm not in the mood."

"I brought you some Ding Dongs in case you get hungry." Her enemy smiled and shoved an individually wrapped package of cream-filled chocolate cakes in her face.

The stench of plastic smoke shocked Tricia with its intensity. She gagged and turned away from the pastry. Brynn laughed, but it sounded strange, kind of a strangled chuckle. Tricia looked at her. She was gulping for air, short croaks that did nothing to fill her lungs.

"What's wrong, Brynn?"

The teen clutched her throat. Her face was turning red. Her expression had changed from humor to horror. She dropped the package of cupcakes and stumbled back into the lockers. She frantically pointed at her throat. Her face darkened. Her eyes bulged with terror.

Tricia realized what was happening to her. She grabbed Brynn's arm and spun her around to face the other way. She put both arms around her waist, jammed a fist into her solar plexus, just under her rib cage. She said a quick prayer and squeezed upward. She heard a gurgling pop and the wet wad of gray gum slapped against the locker room wall.

Brynn sucked in a huge shuddering breath. She smiled weakly and shook her head. "I don't know what happened. I was laughing and then I couldn't breathe." She rubbed her throat.

"You gonna be okay?" Tricia asked.

"Yeah." She rubbed her throat again. "That was super scary."

"No doubt. I'm glad I remembered how to do that Heimlich thing."

Deadly Diet

Brynn looked at her, her eyes wide with shock. "Tricia, y-you just saved my life."

"Well, I just, you know, saw you were in trouble, and..." She didn't know what else to say, especially when Brynn started to cry. Seeing her tormentor reduced to tears left her with ambiguous feelings. She was glad to see that Brynn was capable of regret but also realized that it had taken a brush with death to do it.

"None of this would've happened if I hadn't been trying to piss you off," Brynn cried. "I'm so sorry."

"I'm just glad you're okay." It was a trite thing to say, but she could think of nothing else.

Brynn pressed the tears into her cheeks with the heel of her hand. "I've been such a hag to you ever since you started at Bitterbrook, I'm surprised you didn't let me turn blue and keel over."

Tricia shrugged.

"I'm really sorry," Brynn said, looking down at the floor. She took a deep breath and sighed. "I hope you can forgive me."

"Does this mean our feud's over?"

Brynn nodded, picked up the cupcake, and tossed it into a nearby trashcan. "Over." She smiled and extended her hand. "Shake on it?"

She took her hand and said, "All over."

After they exchanged an awkward hug, the girls stood there for a moment, neither one of them knowing what to do next.

Brynn said, "Guess we'd better get to class. We have to go out to the softball fields today. We're playing kickball." No wonder Tricia hadn't seen Tomoko in the gym.

She grabbed her jacket. "In the cold drizzle? Mustache Milton is inhuman."

"It's only fifty something and she calls it a mist. Coach says girls need to toughen up."

"Like I said, inhuman." She followed Brynn out of the door. Mustache Milton blew her whistle and called everyone to form lines for calisthenics.

As she and Brynn approached the softball diamond, Tricia saw Tomoko standing in the back row of the calisthenics formation. She locked eyes with her before the Japanese girl looked away.

"Well, thanks so much again," Brynn said, then added, "Girl, a thank you sounds so weak for saving my life, but I mean it."

"I just did what I had to."

Brynn smiled and put her hand on her shoulder. "I'm not gonna forget it. I swear." She ran and joined her friends in the front row. Tricia could tell she was telling them about what had just happened.

Having ended her stint as a hero, the problem of the noxious odor coming from a cupcake wrapped in plastic confronted her. How could she have smelled the pastry through the wrap? She couldn't, which led her to believe that the mere sight of food had triggered the smoky smell. And if that was true, how the hell did it work? She had to find Tomoko and get some answers.

She walked to where Tomoko was standing. She squeezed between her and Lucinda, a girl she knew from Math class. "Hey, Tomoko, I need to talk to you about the you-know… things." I didn't want to say, "pills," in case Lucinda overheard and got the wrong idea.

"We cannot talk now," she said quickly. "Class is starting."

"I really need to find out some stuff."

Tomoko managed a wavering smile. "After class."

Coach blew her whistle to start the calisthenics. Tricia's stomach grumbled in protest of the bouncing jumping jacks that stirred it up.

After the girls finished warming up, the coach picked teams for kickball. Tricia hoped to land on the same team as Tomoko so that they would have a chance to talk during the team's at-bats, but Mustache Milton divided them into teams of eleven and Tomoko ended up on the other team.

The coach got behind the plate to umpire. "Okay, Team one, take the field. Team two, you're up."

Tricia trotted out to play shortstop where she had more of a chance of getting the ball kicked to her. With the way her stomach was acting, she needed the distraction. Mustache Milton rolled a burnt-sienna-colored ball to the pitcher, Pam Wilson, and the game began.

Deadly Diet

During the first inning, Tomoko came to bat and kicked the ball into left field. As she ran around first base to stretch the single into a double, the left fielder Lucinda threw her the ball. Tricia turned and fired it at Tomoko to put her out. She missed her. Tomoko saw the chance to advance to third but tripped on second base and tumbled to the red clay. Lisa Mason, the first baseman, had caught her miss and hit her with the ball. Out! Tomoko rose slowly. She brushed herself off and took a step toward the sidelines. She cried out and started to hop on one leg to take the pressure off her right ankle. Mustache Milton chugged over and offered a beefy shoulder. Tomoko leaned against her and the two left the playing field. The coach transferred her burden to Mini-Milt and then assumed her role as umpire again.

As Tricia watched the assistant coach and Tomoko run a slow three-legged race toward the locker room, she hoped that Mini-Milt tended to her injured friend so that Tomoko could watch the rest of the game from the dugout, providing Tricia with the perfect opportunity to talk with her, but the Japanese girl never returned.

After the game was over, her team won by two runs, Tricia ran to the locker room to get showered and dressed. She was hoping to catch Tomoko before she made it to her next class, but she couldn't find her. She must have gone to the clinic.

The bell rang for lunch, and Tricia walked to the cafeteria. Horf was sitting at their usual table waiting for her. He waved and she pointed toward the line to let him know she was ordering something to eat. Tricia was ravenous. Smells drifted by her, but to her surprise, there was no accompanying odor of smoke, just the aroma of meat loaf with gravy, French fries, and broiled hamburgers. The physical activity of the kickball game must have driven the last vestiges of the pill from her system.

She didn't understand. Tomoko had told her last night that one pill per day was all she needed to take. So, was her extra poundage diluting the ingredients? Should she have taken two pills? And where the hell was her *Hangakira*? So many questions, so few answers.

Her stomach growled to hurry up and feed it.

The smell of Bitterbrook High's version of the Burger King Whopper tempted her. She could taste the juicy beef, the sweet onion, the pickles, the iceberg lettuce, the ketchup, and the creamy mayonnaise. One little burger wasn't going to hurt anything. Half a burger. No, a quarter. Just one bite. Two max.

No.

No!

NO! How many times am I going to play this game of portions with myself?

She snapped open her purse and pulled the drawstring on the pouch of pills to open it. She snagged a tablet and asked the girl behind her to hold her place. She nodded and Tricia hurried to the nearest water fountain. She took the pill and returned to her place in the line.

As she drew closer to the food display, her desire for the burger waned, but without the accompanying smoky stench. When the time came for her selection, she was a good girl and ordered the fruit salad. For a change, the chunks of cantaloupe and watermelon, apple slices, and strawberries looked really fresh.

The woman at the register took her money and Tricia went to sit with Horf. She sniffed the fruit but didn't smell anything off-putting. The pills only intensified the smell of cooked food.

"Fruit salad," Horf said. "Nice."

She sat at the table. "Yeah, sticking to the plan."

He smiled and spun a wad of whole wheat spaghetti noodles onto his plastic fork.

She put her tray down on the table and unfolded a napkin. A disturbing chill that she recognized as the side effect of the pill shuddered through her.

Horf stuffed his oversized bite of spaghetti into his mouth. A blop of sauce sat on his chin like a slimy blood-red mole. She felt a quiver of disgust, so she reached over and dabbed the splotch with her napkin.

"Thanks," he said. "I heard you saved Brynn or something. I heard her and her goon squad talking in line about it."

She told him what had happened.

"Blown chance," was all he said.

84

Deadly Diet

Tricia laughed and stabbed a strawberry with her fork. Red juice spilled from its side. She lifted it to her mouth and sniffed the sweet fruit. Still no plastic smoke smell. She popped the berry into her mouth, chewed it and almost gagged. She tugged a white napkin from the dispenser and spat the mangled fruit into it. "Damn it!"

"What's wrong?"

"This strawberry's rotten."

"Gross. It looks fine but sometimes you can't tell with fruit."

The napkin holding the juicy strawberry resembled a bloody sheet placed over a murder victim. She tried a few chunks of repellant cantaloupe and some super bitter watermelon before her appetite keeled over and died. Was this what she had to look forward to for the next couple of weeks? Smoke and rot.

Horf's voice interrupted her reverie. "Earth to Tricia."

"Huh?"

"I said, do you want to go to the movies tonight? It's Friday."

"Oh, yeah, sure. Friday at the draft house."

"I thought we'd check out that new horror flick."

"The one about the goblin child?"

"Yeah, *What's Wrong with the Baby*? I read the book and saw the preview. It looks pretty fricking awesome."

She pushed the plate of fruit away from her. "Deal, but you have to let me hold your hand when I get scared."

"So, you can grind my knuckles together like you always do? No thanks. I couldn't hold a fork for days after your last gorilla girl grip."

"I'll use your arm instead."

"Oh, the claw treatment. I still have bruises."

"Why do you take me to these scary flicks if you get hurt so much?"

Horf laughed. "Are you kidding? Watching you cower and cringe is usually better than the movie. I especially love it when you cover your eyes with your hands."

"I'll show you. I won't even blink tonight."

Horf laughed again. "I'll pick you up at seven. The show starts at seven thirty."

"I'll be ready."

"And bring a cross and some holy water just in case there's a redcap goblin hunting us down in the theater. Oh, hey, check this out," Horf said. He showed her the prong of his belt buckle which he had inserted two holes down from the distorted hole into which he had been buckling it. "Two inches gone."

"That's great," she said, noticing for the first time just how much Horf had changed in the past two weeks. In addition to the reduction of his waistline, there were traces of muscle in his arms. She could see the beginning of a firm jawline. Funny, she hadn't noticed what a handsome face he had before.

FIFTEEN

Tricia glanced at the clock on the top of her dresser and saw that it was past six. She put the dystopian novel she'd been trying to read for the past hour on the bedstand and swung her legs to the floor. Before she got ready to go to the movies, she called Tomoko one more time trying to find out if there was some kind of drug in the pills that was causing the bad smells and tastes.

She answered on the third ring.

"Tomoko?"

"Tricia, what's up?"

"Holly?"

"Yeah, hey. Uh, Tomoko can't come to the phone right now. So, hey, how'd you do on the chem test the other day?"

"I got a ninety-seven. Why can't she come to the phone?"

"I need to start sitting by you in class. I got a seventy-two."

"Holly, why can't Tomoko talk?"

There was enough of a pause to tell her that Tomoko was brushing her off. "She's in the shower. Can she call you back?"

"Sure. I'm leaving at around seven to go to the movies. She can call me any time before then."

"Oh, okay, sure."

Tricia decided to do a little investigation. "So, how's Tomoko's ankle?"

"Her ankle?"

"Yeah, she hurt it playing kickball today."

"I guess it must be fine. She didn't mention anything about it and she's not limping."

"Cool," she said. "I'm glad she's okay. I'll see you on Monday at school. And do your chemistry assignments."

She hung up the phone. Why was Tomoko being so evasive, acting as if she'd injured her ankle, and now pretending to be in the shower so she wouldn't have to talk to Tricia? What was she hiding from her? She doubted she'd find out anytime soon. If Tomoko returned the phone call, Tricia would eat her scrunchie.

The phone rang.

"Tricia, this is Tomoko. You called me?"

She wondered how many calories were in an elastic hair tie. "Oh, yeah, I, uh, wanted to ask you about the pills."

"You took one today?"

"Actually two."

"One is all you need. You have questions about their side effects." It was a statement, not a question.

"Yeah, I do. Like, why do I get chills and smell smoke, and why do some things taste funny?"

"Did you not want to lose weight?" Tomoko asked tersely.

"Yeah."

"This is how the pills work. I do not know what's in them. I did not ask. I took them and I lost weight. I am not in bad health. I feel wonderful. Do not question the properties of the pills and they will work for you. Now I have to go."

"But..."

Tomoko hung up.

She started to redial her number but set her phone on the bed. On second thought, she didn't blame Tomoko for being mad at her. She had pestered her into giving her the pills and now that she'd started taking them, she was acting as if she didn't want them. So, the pills made food unpleasant. Big deal. How was that any different from taking diet pills that cut your appetite or made you feel full? The principle was the same: you don't eat, you lose weight. Simple. Were the pills harsh medicine? The harshest. But did they work? Absolutely. She didn't need to know how or why as long as she was cutting calories from her diet. Once she got down to the weight she wanted to be, she would stop taking them and work on staying at that weight. Isn't that exactly what she had been hoping to do all along?

"Tricia, come and eat," Mom called.

Dinner consisted of blackened pork chops, charred potatoes, burnt green beans, and for dessert, spoiled lemon meringue pie. Tricia drank water and choked down a couple of pieces of bland bread.

"Tricia, is that all you're going to eat?" Mom asked. "You're gonna get sick if you don't eat."

"I ate a big lunch today," she said. Three chunks of repugnant cantaloupe and some harsh watermelon. "Horf and I are going to the movies at the draft house. I'll get something there."

"Something healthy, I hope."

"Can I be excused?" She huffed. "I have to get ready."

Mom sighed and told her to go ahead.

Promptly at seven, Horf's car pulled into the driveway and before he could get out, Tricia was running out the front door and heading for his beat-up Nissan Sentra.

"You ready to get scared?" Horf asked with a devious smile.

"Not tonight, bucko," I said snapping her seatbelt.

Horf chuckled menacingly. "We shall see."

He backed the car out of the driveway and headed down the road. At the light, he turned left instead of right which would have taken them directly to the theater.

"Where are you going?" Tricia asked.

"I need to stop at work to pick up my paycheck and cash it. Contrary to widely held belief, my good looks do not get me into the movies for free."

Five minutes later, they pulled into the parking lot of Cornucopia, the market where he worked. He parked and jettisoned his seat belt. "Are you coming?"

"Sure," she said.

As Horf went to the office to pick up his paycheck, Tricia stopped at the magazine rack near the deli. She snagged a copy of CosmoGirl and leafed through it to pass the time.

"This look like a library to you, miss," a man with a gruff voice said. It was Mr. Grunion, Horf's boss. He was a beefy slab of a man with a greasy combover hairstyle, a wide out-of-fashion tie and a shirt that looked as if it was waiting for a stain. He held a meatball sub in one hand and a soda in the other.

She shivered and gasped.

Things were moving inside his sandwich.

"You deef or sumpin? Put the magazine back on the rack or get out the green to pay for it."

The stench of decay hit her in the face.

"The cashier is that way," Grunion said. "Best head there or we're gonna have us a problem."

She gagged and backed away from him, still holding the magazine. She stared at the maggots boiling from the tomato sauce inside his sub and threw the mag at them. Grunion instinctively tried to catch it and bobbled the sandwich which fell to the floor, spilling the larva-infested meatballs across the polished terrazzo. He cursed her. "You're gonna pay for that."

She grabbed a ten out of her purse and flung it toward him. Adult flies emerged from the maggots and buzzed toward her. The stench was garbage piled on top of trash ladled with sewage. She ran out of the building and didn't stop until she had reached Horf's Sentra.

He came out a short time later. "Where'd you go?"

"It was kind of chilly in there." And terrifying.

"Yeah, Grunion keeps it cold. Says the produce doesn't go bad until people get it home. Speaking of The Grunn, you should have seen him a minute ago. Some girl really had him steaming."

"Sorry I missed it. Can we go?"

Deadly Diet

Horf tucked his wallet into his pants and started the car. "Money in pocket. Tricia in car. Let's go find out what's wrong with the baby."

They arrived at Cinematicafé and found seats at their favorite table in the middle of the theater. Horf claimed it was the best spot in which to experience the picture and sound the way the filmmakers intended. They took their seats. She asked Horf if he would wait until the second half of the movie before he ordered his popcorn, no butter, and diet Cherry Coke. He agreed.

The movie opened with the Martin family driving across the rain-drenched moors of Scotland. The director chose not to play any background music during the family's trip to Castle Drochil, and his choice of ominous silence gave the film a sense of realism that tensed her up right away. The film maintained that tension all the way to the family's return to Florida where the mother Vicki gave birth to her miracle baby that had somehow survived a miscarriage that took his twin brother.

As they had agreed, Horf ordered his snack from the server, a petite pregnant girl who probably shouldn't have been watching a movie about a woman giving birth to a monstrous goblin. Tricia asked her for a bottle of spring water.

Fifteen minutes later, she arrived with their order and an apology. The cook had accidentally put butter on the popcorn, so she had to wait for him to pop another batch. To make up for the inconvenience, she handed Horf an extra-large tub of popcorn and a super-sized soda.

As the evil baby Darian stalked his mother into the bathroom where she was preparing to take her bath, Tricia sipped her water and endured the reek of charred popcorn and rancid cherries. She tried to hide from the stench by sitting low in her chair and covering her nose with the collar of her sweater, but the scorched, rotten smell filled the back of her throat with sickness. She rose out of her seat into a slump to keep from blocking the screen, swallowed, and whispered, "Bathroom."

Horf smiled. "Told you." He clucked like a chicken.

"I'll be back."

Horf kept clucking.

Sitting behind them, a man with wild curly hair and thick glasses hissed, "Knock it off, Chicken Little."

Horf zipped his lip and, with a smug grin stuck to his face, waved goodbye.

She ignored him, hunched, and stumbled in her effort to get out of the theater. She opened the double doors and the server carrying a tray of nachos and cheese with jalapeno slices passed her. A cloud of stinging stink slammed her backward. Her stomach lurched.

She looked toward the concession stand where a steel beetle was laying yellowish-white eggs that tumbled into a clear bin. The concession worker ran a scoop through the maggoty-colored eggs and dumped them into a tub. He squirted viscous snot from the faucet of a plastic container. Tricia gagged and turned from the sight.

"Have to get out of here," she whispered.

Taking a deep breath with her mouth only, she staggered through the exit door and stumbled out into the fresh frigid air.

As soon as she stepped outside, the smell vanished.

She couldn't believe how strong the pill was still acting. She sat heavily on the concrete steps leading to the ticket booth and waited until the sickness subsided.

A brief time later, Horf came out of the theater looking for her.

"Hey, chicken, are you coming back in or what?" Horf said.

"In a minute. I feel kinda queasy."

Horf's concern replaced his grin. "Are you okay?"

"Yeah. Go ahead and watch the movie. I'll join you in a little bit."

"You sure? A soda will help settle your stomach."

"I'll be all right. Go ahead and watch the movie. I know you've been wanting to see it. I don't mind."

"If you're sick, maybe we should go."

"No, really, I'll be fine. Go. I'll be there in a minute."

"Okay." Horf shrugged. "But if you start feeling worse, come in and get me and I'll take you home."

She nodded.

Horf went back into the theater leaving her to contemplate the lasting effects of the pills. She waited until she estimated he had

Deadly Diet

finished his popcorn and drink before returning to their table. Thankfully, his food was gone.

He leaned and whispered in her ear. "Feeling better?"

She nodded, although she wasn't so sure how convincing she was.

Horf looked at her skeptically. "You sure you just weren't scared?"

"You got me. I was, but I'm over it now."

"Good, because I hear the last act of the movie will make your skin crawl."

"Will you two can the chatter?" the curly-haired man sitting behind them said louder than need be.

Horf zipped his lip again. They settled back into their seats to finish watching the movie.

When Tricia got home, she undressed and trudged into the bathroom to get ready for bed. Once again, the scale glowered at her with piercing red eyes. She tapped the button with her toe and the thing's eyes blinked before revealing the double zero. She stepped on the scale. It flashed a few times and then revealed that she had lost one pound! In one day!

"All right!" She thrust her fist into the air to celebrate.

She bounced off the scale and danced into her room.

"One pound in one day. Now, that's progress," she said. "If I keep going at this rate, I'll be where I want to be in no time."

Smiling, she glanced in the full-length mirror at her minus-one-pound body. Behind her stood an ancient Asian woman glaring at her.

Tricia's breath left her.

She turned quickly but found no one standing there watching her.

She looked back into the mirror and stared at the reflection of a confused, frightened teenager who happened to look just like her. She shook her head. She glanced at the dresser where she kept her secret stash and thought maybe she should quit taking them until she found out what was in them causing her to hallucinate.

Her gaze shifted to the bathroom scale that had just revealed her one-pound-in-one-day weight loss. *A pound in a day! Who cares if there's a mild hallucinogenic in the pills?* As long as she could tell that the visions, sounds, and smells weren't real, she would keep taking the pills until she reached her goal weight of 105 pounds. At the time, she didn't care if she saw a ravenous ten-foot-tall Kit-Kat bar advancing toward her to make a snack of her, she was gonna lose this weight.

SIXTEEN

Tricia woke early the next morning with the distinct impression that someone was standing over her. She tried to open her eyes to see who was there but was unable to move. As she tried to break through the sleep paralysis, the pressure inside her built to an uncomfortable level. She gasped and jerked to a seated position. The spell broken.

She stared wide-eyed into the room and waited for her pupils to adjust to the darkness. Familiar objects cast in shadow seemed to conceal secrets best left unspoken. Her scalp prickled at the thought she was not alone.

"Mom," she whispered, thinking that she had come to wake her for their morning jog. "You there?"

Her mother did not answer.

Tricia squinted at the clock and saw that it was four A.M. It would be an hour and a half before her mother would come to get her for their run.

Had Penny gotten scared and snuck into her room again? She called out her name. There was no response.

She put her head back on the pillow, closed her eyes, and tried to get back to sleep.

But she couldn't shake the feeling that someone was there in the room with her. She made the mistake of looking one last time. The ancient Asian woman she had seen in the mirror now stood in the shadows of the closet. She could see pinpoints of reflected streetlight in her milky eyes. The old woman was staring straight at her.

Tricia couldn't breathe. She tried to call out to her mom and dad, but her mouth was dry as dust.

The woman stood there, watching her, unmoving. Her gaunt face unnerved her. Pale skin stretched tight over sunken cheeks. Blackened teeth locked in a grimace could have been a smile or the rictus of death. She was wearing a white silk kimono. Her silent observance disturbed her more than any moving specter could.

Are ghosts real, Trisha Wisha?

The roaring vortex inside her mind made her head feel as if it were coming off her neck. She clutched her pillow to her chest, a life preserver against the swirling waters of terror that threatened to swamp her.

Again, she tried to call out for help, but could only manage a dry croak.

The woman didn't move but was radiating intent to do her harm.

She swallowed dust and whispered, "Daddy, help me."

The hag didn't stir. She just glared at her with those glittering eyes so contemptuous toward her. Tricia whimpered. The corners of the woman's eyes turned up in a smile.

"Dad," she managed to cry a little louder than a whisper.

The fans of the central heater clicked on. The abrupt sound made her cry out.

Frantically, she looked around the room and saw the lamp beside her bed.

The light!

Light dispelled evil.

The specter must have read her mind. She flew from the closet toward her, her kimono swirling behind her as if blown by a supernatural wind.

Deadly Diet

"No!" Tricia cried. She rolled to the side of the bed, reached over, and slapped on the light. Fingernails of pain jabbed her in the eyes. She blinked once, then again. Her eyes adjusted and she looked toward the closet.

The spirit was still there, a scarecrow of a woman composed of hanging dresses and blouses. Her eyes were glossy mother-of-pearl buttons on a shirt pocket. Her gaunt face was the folds of the blouse.

"Tricia."

She jumped at the sound of the voice. "You ready to go?"

It was her mother.

Tricia looked at the clock and saw that it was five-thirty. She must have fallen asleep and dreamed of the ghost. She laughed.

"What's so funny?"

"Nothing. Just a little dream I had."

"What was it about?"

"A girl who was afraid of her clothes," she said.

"Sounds Brothers Grimm to me." Mom shrugged. "Get ready to go. Mrs. Alquist will be waiting."

She got out of bed and looked into the closet again. "Boo," she said, jumping at the clothes ghost.

She dressed and didn't think about the woman in the closet again.

SEVENTEEN

Twelve pounds in one week! Her weight loss was beyond her wildest expectations. In that time, Tricia had grown used to the constant hunger, sudden chills and the disturbing reactions to food that kept her from eating. She had even convinced her mom that she had taken up intermittent fasting, showing her the studies that demonstrated its benefits, so she could avoid eating dinner. She did find that she could choke down oatmeal with milk for breakfast, drink plenty of liquids, and take the right vitamins and minerals, so she wasn't totally starving herself. Occasionally, the revolting sights and smells would overwhelm her senses and shut her down, and at those times, she thought it might be a clever idea to stop taking the pills for a little while, just to clear her system. But each time, she recovered her composure, grateful for having averted a setback in her diet plan.

She stepped lightly off the scale in the locker room at school and stood in front of the mirror. She tried to determine from what part of her the twelve pounds had come. Her face and arms were definitely thinner, but she could still see plenty of fat on her butt and abdomen.

Deadly Diet

And then there were the dreaded saddlebags on her thighs. Yutch. If she kept going the way she was, it wouldn't be long before those bag girls disappeared.

She was pleased with her progress. At this rate, in less than two weeks, she would reach her goal, then no more pills. She wished she could tell Tomoko how well she was doing, but she hadn't been at school all week. Tricia tried calling her, but she never answered her phone. She wondered if something might have happened to her. If Tomoko were ill, the news of Tricia's weight loss might cheer her up since she'd given her the pills that were responsible for her excellent results.

Mustache Milton came out of her office, startling her. "Why aren't you dressed and at lunch?"

"Sorry. I, uh, I'm running a little late."

"Well, hurry up so I can lock up and get to lunch myself. Got to stoke the furnace."

Tricia nodded and hustled to her locker. As she dressed, she asked Coach Milton if she had heard anything about Tomoko.

The coach closed an open locker. "She's gone to be with her grandfather in New York. He's real sick from what she said."

"Is she gonna come back to Bitterbrook?"

"I don't know." Mustache Milton looked at her curiously. "What have you been doing lately? You look like you've lost some weight."

"I'm running in the mornings and I'm on a diet."

The coach rubbed her chin. "Hmm. Well, let's go. I'm hungry."

Tricia nodded, closed her locker, and followed her out of the exit.

That afternoon, she called Megan and Mandy to give them a progress report on her weight loss and they got so chatty about how great it was that she almost missed the bus. As she hustled to the stop, she was surprised to see Brynn Alquist smiling and waiting for her.

"Tricia!" she called out, her voice echoing down the almost empty halls. "I've got some great news."

"About what?" she said. The doors of her bus were still open but wouldn't be for long.

"The team. Tomoko called this afternoon and said that she was transferring to another school to move in with her grandpa." Brynn smiled broadly. "Coach Milton had to let her go."

"That's not great news. Tomoko is a friend of mine," she said, offended by Brynn's callous attitude. Despite that fact that she and Brynn had buried the hatchet after the choking incident, she still considered her to be a bit of a bitchy snob. Just because she wasn't picking on her anymore didn't mean she had mended her ways when it came to the way she treated other people. "I have to go before the bus leaves."

"You don't get it. Coach wants you to take Tomoko's place on the team."

"What?"

"She says you were the next-highest-rated dancer who tried out, so you're on the team… if you want to be."

"If I want to be?" She beamed. "Oh, man, this is totally lit." She laughed and pumped her fist. "Does she want me to come to practice today?"

"No, you're not supposed to know until she calls you tonight. She told us before practice. I snuck out to tell you. I thought you might like to hear a sneak preview."

Tricia's smile hurt her cheeks. "This is unreal. I'm on the dance team."

"And we have our first appearance in a month and a half."

"That's great. By then, I'll be down to where I want to be."

"I've been meaning to tell you that I noticed you've lost some weight. You'll have guys stepping on their tongues when you hit your goal." Brynn checked the time on her phone. "I'd better be getting back to practice."

"Thanks again for telling me."

"Gooch. See you tomorrow morning at the bus stop," Brynn replied, and then took off running back to the gymnasium.

She wanted to cheer. So that's why Mustache Milton was so interested in her weight. She must have decided losing the extra twelve pounds made a difference. If that was true, then wait until she saw her at 105! She might make captain!

Deadly Diet

She heard the squeak and clap of the bus doors closing. She ran to stop Earl the driver from leaving by banging on the glass. He pulled the lever and let her in, scolding her with a well-placed frown. He pushed the bar to shut the door again.

She sat in the back, realizing she had a stupid smile on her face and did not care a bit. As the bus rumbled to her stop, she thought of Tomoko and her grandfather's illness and sympathy tempered her elation. After all her challenging work to make the dance team, to be forced to give up her position was a cruel blow. She called her and left a supportive message.

After she got home and put her backpack away, she hustled to the bus stop to walk Penny home. Her little sister marched off the bus, pumping her arms and counting off her numbers.

Tricia excitedly told her about making the dance team. Penny shrugged and kept up her marching count all the way home. Her sister could be a bit of a troll.

After Tricia got Penny safely planted in front of the television, she called Horf and told him the good news as well. He did not react in the way she expected. "She's playing you, Tricia. It's been long enough from the day you saved Brynn for her to have reverted to her true nature as a female dog."

"No way," she said. "You didn't see how happy she was for me. She couldn't fake that."

"Imagine how happy she'll be tomorrow when you tell her that the coach didn't call you."

"You really hate her, don't you?"

"Oh, no, I love someone calling me Horfvomit and finding boogers stuck on her locker all the time. I hope she is pranking you."

"What do you mean?"

"Nothing."

"No, you said you hope she's pranking me. That's harsh."

"I just mean you should be on the team, but not if it means you're going to start hanging out with Brynn and her goon squad."

"Chill, Horf. We're not going to start hanging out," she said. "Can't you just be happy for me making the team?"

"Happy, happy, joy, joy," he said dully.

An uncomfortable silence sat between them.

"Do you really think Brynn could be lying to me?" Tricia asked him.

"Let me put it this way. One time, she called my house and told my mom there had been an accident. Then she said I had been born. What do you think?"

Horf's suspicions about Brynn's treachery lurked in the back of Tricia's mind until Coach Milton called after dinner and made her team membership official. She was now a full-fledged member of the Ravenettes.

Life was good and getting better.

PART TWO

EIGHTEEN

"Today, I'm done," Tricia said. She looked in the mirror, admiring the way her new jeans fit her new slim and trim body. Her thunder thighs were now lightning. The only way she would hear someone call sooey was if she happened to be passing a farm. She slipped on a tight-fitting pink tee with a vee collar to further accentuate her weight loss. Since joining the dance team four weeks ago, she had dropped the remaining twenty-eight pounds and had reached her goal weight. Now she could cut out the pills, say goodbye to the hallucinations, and return to her mother's vegan diet, just as she said she would. A healthy menu, running in the morning, dance drills in the afternoon, this girl was going to stay in shape.

And not a moment too soon. Her lack of proper nourishment had finally caught up with her. For the past week at practice, she had been sluggish and had the attention span of a lobotomized fruit fly, a combo that hadn't sat well with Mustache Milton who had begun calling her

"One Step" as in "One Step Behind." It was a relief that she had reached her goal weight and could now stop the radical diet before she lost her spot on the team.

She looked in the dresser drawer where she kept the pills. "Thank you and good riddance," she said. Tricia wished that Tomoko was still at school so she could thank her. She turned and headed for the dining room, where her first real breakfast in a month waited.

Tricia strolled happily into the room where Mom was putting a big plate of hash brown potatoes, whole wheat toast, and a tofu-scramble on the table. Penny scooped a spoonful of "eggs" and hash browns onto her plate, as did her dad who had shocked the whole family last week when he declared the war between carnivore and vegan was over. Veganism had won. The news delighted her mom who kissed him for a shockingly long time in front of Penny and her. Tricia thought it was adorable. Penny hid her eyes.

"Isn't your outfit a little… tight, Tricia?" Dad said. "I know you're proud of losing weight, but let's not get carried away." He ate a forkful of potatoes.

She rolled her eyes. "I'm wearing a jacket with it."

"Leave her alone, Alan. She's fit," Mom said.

"If you mean in shape, thanks," she replied. "If you're trying to be 'that mom,' major cringe."

Mom laughed. "I meant fit in the most un-teen way possible."

"Yikes meter off then. Oh, and I want you to know that today I'm officially off my diet."

"That's great," Mom said. "I was beginning to worry about you. I even read up on eating disorders to make sure you weren't taking it too far."

"Don't worry. I'm done."

"If you want to keep the weight off, stick with the vegan brigade. I haven't gained one pound back since I went on the program."

"And I dropped a couple," Dad chimed in. "And I don't even miss bacon… much." He wiped an imaginary tear from his eye.

"I plan on doing that," she said. Tricia scooped potatoes on her plate, then poured a small puddle of ketchup next to them. An unpleasant familiar chill swept over her. She grew uneasy. She took a hesitant bite of her breakfast.

The potatoes tasted like dirt.

She swallowed them with difficulty. Damn it. There must be some residue still left in her system from her last dose of pills. With her fork, she stabbed a couple of potatoes and held them close to her nose. She smelled the pungent odor of wet earth, the reek of a leaky coffin. She put the potatoes back onto her plate.

"Something wrong with the tates?" Mom said. "You're not eating them."

"Yes, I am," she said, forcing a forkful of the filthy potatoes into her mouth. She couldn't skip breakfast very well after declaring an end to her diet without raising questions she didn't want to answer. If she told her mom that she was still experiencing effects from unknown, unregulated pills that she had taken for the past five weeks, her mother would whisk her away to the emergency room, and after they got home, bury her in her room for the rest of the school year. She didn't even like her to take aspirin. Stupid fricking pills. How long were they going to stay in her system? She chewed the potatoes, enduring the earthy grit. She clenched her teeth and swallowed the disgusting lump. She smiled wondering if mud covered her teeth.

After she battled her way to a clean plate, she strolled calmly up the stairs and into the bathroom, where she frantically scrubbed the mucky taste from her mouth. She hoped that the remaining residue from the pills would be out of her system by lunchtime. She hustled to her room, gathered her backpack, and headed to the bus stop.

On the ride to school, she sat by herself placing her backpack on the seat next to her to discourage any late breakfast eaters from sitting there. Unfortunately, everyone who rode the bus chose that day to do so. Chester Timbs stood in front of her empty seat huffing until she slid her backpack onto the floor in front of her to make room for him. He slumped into the seat. Chester was the kind of kid that vampires turned into their willing servants in movies. He opened his backpack and, as Tricia dreaded, pulled out something to eat. When she saw it was a gingerbread man cookie, she didn't know whether to laugh or cry. He bit the foot off the gingerbread man, and she shivered at the sight of blood running down Chester's chin. Cold fear sat in the pit of her stomach.

To distract herself, Tricia took out her history book, her notebook, and a pen. She focused on learning about Sherman's march through Georgia during the Civil War, but the overpowering stink of ginger and rot sickened her. Once, she glanced up at Chester just as he bit the head off the screaming Gingerbread Man and blood-red frosting spurted from the cookie's neck onto Chester's shirt. After that, she kept her head down, eyes on her book, until they arrived at school.

She let her stomach settle, waiting for everyone to leave the bus before she stepped off. Awkwardly, she hit the last step wrong-footed and did a little stumble. Her history book and notebook went flying. She bent down to grab her book just as a hand closed around the spine. She looked up into the eyes of Trey Curtis.

"You look like you could use some help," he said, handing her the book.

She smiled and felt her cheeks redden. "Thanks a lot," she replied.

He picked up her notebook and gave it to her. Tricia stuck the books into her backpack and started to walk toward her locker.

"Thanks a lot," she repeated, struck dumb as in "Duh, I can't think of anything else to say."

"No problem, Tricia," he replied.

Tricia? Did Trey Curtis just say my name?

He smiled a hundred-watt smile. "So, did you do that Algebra homework last night? Man, what a pain."

"I know, right. I barely got through it."

He nodded. "A real pain."

"Yeah."

She smiled and tried not to giggle like a lovesick fool. "Well, I better get to class." Social scientists will study why she said that for decades, but Trey didn't let it bother him. He walked with her in the direction of her locker. She hoped her wobbly knees would hold up.

"So, Tricia, you're on the dance team, right?"

She smiled. "Yeah, I've been practicing with the team for about four weeks."

Deadly Diet

"Must be tough work. You're in really great shape."

She blushed, dumbstruck by the compliment. Trey didn't notice as he was looking at his reflection in a classroom window, fixing his hair. Tricia finally managed to respond, "It's a workout for sure, plus, I run six miles in the mornings with my mom and Mrs. Alquist." *Too much detail, Tricia, but at least you left out the part about taking mind-altering pills that made food look, taste and smell like death warmed over.*

They arrived at her locker.

"I'll see you in class," Trey said. "Since you, no doubt, get better grades than I do, maybe we can study together sometime."

Her brain short-circuited. Did the absolute top of her list of teen-dreamy boyfriends just ask her to study with him? That was one step away from asking her out on a date. She opened her locker and put her books away.

"Well, do you want to or not?" Trey asked.

"Huh?" Tricia said.

"You want to study together sometime?"

"Oh, uh, yeah, that would be amazing. I mean I'd like that," she said.

"Cool, then I'll see you in second period."

As Trey walked away, Tricia saw Horf pass him and amble toward her. When he came within earshot, she gushed, "You won't believe what just happened to me."

"That's one phrase I never understood. You won't believe blah, blah, woof, woof. I mean if I'm not going to believe it, why bother telling me?"

She shook her head. "You're in rare form."

"And you are in great shape, so if you're going to tell me that I won't believe that you just weighed yourself and you hit your ideal weight, I will say, I can see that."

"No, this is more unbelievable than that."

"You just discovered you have an extra bone in your head."

"Be serious." Her smile was infectious.

The grinning Horf shrugged. "I give up then. What is it?"

"Trey Curtis asked me to study with him."

The smile froze on his face. "Oh, really."

"I can't believe it. I'm on a roll. First, I make the dance team, then I lose the weight, and now a guy that didn't know I even existed has asked me to study with him."

"I'm glad for you," Horf replied, decidedly not.

"Thanks." she beamed, clueless to his feelings.

"I lost another couple of pounds myself," he said. He pressed his palm against the front of his shirt to reveal his flat torso. "And I bench-pressed one-eighty-five for the first time."

"I can't believe it ..." Tricia bubbled.

"I was a little surprised myself."

"... Trey Curtis actually asked me to do something with him! People are starting to pay attention to me and one of them is the best-looking guy at Bitterbrook High."

Horf deflated before her eyes, but at that moment, she didn't notice or care. He puffed himself back up and replied, "Yep, Trey's the closest thing we have to Albert Einstein here at BBH. Of course, that would be Albert Einstein the dumbo octopus in the fish tank in Mr. Hearn's biology class."

"Don't shade Trey. You don't even know him."

"And you do?"

"We'd better get to class," she said. "I'm already in Coach Milton's doghouse and a detention might put me under it. Just one thing, Horf. If anything comes out of me and Trey studying together, I want you to know you're still my bestest and that will never change."

"And if I believe that, I have an acre of swampland between my ears to sell myself."

She kissed his cheek. "Put a hold on that check. I swear here and now, I'm never going to ghost you."

"You don't have to tell me that, Tricia."

"Why is that?"

"Because I don't believe in ghosts." He waved and headed for his first period class before he remembered something and turned back toward her. "Oh, hey, before I forget, I've got two tickets to the concert at the Elemental for Friday. Unhinged Mimes is playing and Sleeping Vermin. Wanna go instead of our usual movie night?"

Deadly Diet

"Yeah, that sounds cool. I haven't been to a concert in a long time. It should be fun."

NINETEEN

Lunch sucked: chills, earwax tomatoes, lettuce as bitter as quinine, carrots infested with weevils. There was even a brief appearance of the Asian woman that haunted Tricia's nightmares. She was starting to get the feeling that she had done something irrevocably bad to her brain by taking the pills Tomoko had given her. She might have to revoke her thank-you and replace it with a curse. She pushed a cherry tomato around her plate, trying to muster the courage to stab it with her fork and try to eat it.

"I thought you told me you stopped dieting," Horf said. "In case you didn't know, the food you have in front of you is uneaten." He took a bite of his chickpea salad sandwich.

"I am off the diet, Horf, it's just…" She dropped her fork onto her plate and huffed in frustration. "It's just that I… I…"

"It's just that you… you… what? Tell me what's going on."

For the longest moment, she stared at the ceiling before she sighed, looked at Horf and coughed up the truth about the pills.

"That's fricking great," he said. "Taking pills that frick up your brain. That's some diet plan you and Tomoko worked up. No wonder she left school. She didn't want you to file a lawsuit against her."

"I stopped taking them last night, but there must still be some in my system. I mean I can't get my appetite back. Food just... Yutch. I can't stand to look at it, smell it, or taste it."

"How do these pills work?"

She shrugged. "I just know that they do."

"Apparently, they work like a charm," Horf said. "Too bad, that charm is a voodoo doll. That was really, really dumb, taking pills for five weeks without knowing what was in them."

"Hey, I reached my goal way faster than doing it with the vegan diet, made the dance team, and Trey Curtis is asking me to study with him, so I don't think that's too really, really dumb."

"And what if the pills permanently damaged your brain?"

Her stomach lurched at the idea that he could be right. Her next words belied her nervousness. "I'm sure it's just temporary until I flush the excess out of my system."

Horf took her hand. "Tricia, I want you to promise me you won't take any more of those pills, even if you put back on a few pounds."

"Hey, with dance practice and running, I won't be gaining any weight. And I'm happy, too. I don't need cakes and cookies and ice cream to make me feel better. Everything's going just as I planned. Believe me, I'm off those things for good."

"Okay, if you've got it under control," Horf said.

"I do," she said. She looked at her uneaten lunch and bit her bottom lip.

"Hey, Tricia," Brynn Alquist called from across the room. "Come here for a second."

"What does she want?" Horf asked. "Jeez, ever since you joined the team, she's been trying to get you into her squad just like I said would happen."

"She's okay," Tricia said. "In small doses."

"Like the bubonic plague," Horf added.

She smiled and replied, "Back in a sec."

She got up from the table and walked over to where Brynn and Cathi were sitting. Brynn smiled coyly and took a sip of her drink. "Trey Curtis has been talking about you."

"What?"

"Cathi's boyfriend says Trey's been talking about you," Brynn looked at her friend. "Tell her, Cath."

"That's right," Cathi said. "Dane told me that since you lost so much weight, Trey's been talking about you a lot."

Tricia's stomach tingled. "Get out."

"Dane thinks he likes you."

"No way." She laughed in disbelief.

"That's what he said," Cathi replied.

"Anyway, I just thought you'd like to know," Brynn said.

"I would, I mean I do. Thanks."

"Why don't you stay here and sit with us?" Brynn said, looking at Horf with restrained contempt.

"No, thanks. My lunch is over there."

Brynn nodded. "If you ever want to sit with us instead of Horfvomit—sorry, Horf —there's always a seat." She smiled and started gabbing to her friends again.

All of a sudden, she got the uneasy feeling that Brynn and Cathi were playing a joke on her.

But that didn't ring true. She and Cathi had been consistently nice to her at practice, despite the fact that for the past week she had been making the team repeat routines because of her fatigue-driven mistakes. So, Trey did like her. He did ask her to study with him, and today in class, he had been talkative, even flirtatious. Her stomach fluttered. Trey Curtis and Tricia Hall, Bitterbrook's newest couple?

She floated back to the table and joined Horf.

"What are you smiling about?" he asked.

"Brynn says that Trey Curtis likes me."

Horf looked down at his plate. "Yay."

"Why can't you just be happy for me?"

"I am happy for you. See?" With his fingertips, he pushed up the corners in his mouth to approximate a phony smile. "And I'll be even happier when you realize what a narciopath Trey Curtis is and curb

114

him." He finished his sandwich in what she could only describe as angry bites.

They sat in silence for the rest of the lunch period and didn't talk to each other again until the middle of sixth period when Horf leaned over and said, "Did you see on Reddit where a cat was killed when it googled the word curiosity?"

"Yeah," she said. "Now it's down to eight lives."

They nodded solemnly, and with that, were cool once again.

She spent the rest of her school day trying to focus her fuzzy attention on her teachers who were speaking a different language.

At dance practice that afternoon, her inability to concentrate continued to plague her. She flubbed her way through the routines, earning the team extra laps. When Mustache Milton finally blew her whistle and announced that it was time for a break, Tricia was ready to give up. She ran over to the cooler to get some Gatorade in the hopes that it would restore some bounce to her step and cool her off. She poured herself a large cup and sat on the bleachers. Brynn joined her.

"That last routine is a beeyotch," Brynn said, gulping her drink. "You think you're going to get it?"

"Yeah, I'll get it. Sorry about the laps," she replied. A shudder of chills spread over her. She wiped her brow and took a sip of the lemon-lime-flavored drink. "Ugh." She spat the drink back into the cup. It tasted like water from a stagnant pond.

"What's wrong?"

"Um, there was a bug in my drink."

"Want me to get you another?" Brynn asked. "I'm going back for a refill."

"No, thanks. I'll just get a drink of water."

"Suit yourself."

She ran over to the fountain and stooped for a cool drink of water. It refreshed her and tasted fine, but the change in her body temperature sent another chill through her.

When she stood, she saw a face glaring at her from the small square window of the gym door. It was the Asian woman, but she looked younger than before, closer to her fifties than eighties. She gazed at

Tricia, absolutely still, with these cold dark eyes under smudges of charcoal that had replaced her shaved eyebrows. She smiled and it was more terrifying than anything else about her. It wasn't her blackened teeth that made her smile so awful, it was the wickedness, the absolute wickedness, spewing from that grin. Tricia closed her eyes, opened them and the woman was gone.

Those damned pills. Those fricking damned pills. When was she going to be free from the hallucinations they caused? And why did she keep seeing this same vision of an Asian woman?

She trudged back to where the team had gathered to review the troublesome parts of their routine. Try as she might, she couldn't get that woman's evil face out of her mind. The utter wickedness of her expression left her wondering what trauma in her life had caused her to experience such a vision of cruelty. She looked over her shoulder at the window of the gym door.

"Tricia, pay attention," Mustache Milton snapped. "You're one of the girls that's not getting it."

She couldn't answer. She was paralyzed by the sight of the wicked woman glaring at her again. What Tricia saw on her face was nothing less than murder.

"Tricia Hall, are you listening?"

A slow blackened smile crept across the woman's face. Tricia heard her voice inside her head. *"Anata wa tabemasen." You will not eat.*

"All right, Miss Head in the Clouds, hit the showers and think about what it means to you to be on this team."

The woman in her vision shimmered and vanished. She snapped to attention. "What?"

"You heard me. If you're not going to listen, we don't want you wasting our time."

"What?"

"Go on, and don't let the door hit you on the butt on the way out."

"But Coach…" I'm hallucinating like a tourist on ayahuasca, she wanted to say.

"Go!"

Go? Really? Go to where that murderous evil specter conjured up by my poisoned brain is waiting for me. No thanks.

116

Deadly Diet

"Tricia Hall! Get moving!"

She took a deep breath and gathered her composure. "Coach, I'm sorry. I just... Sorry."

"Go!"

More frightened than embarrassed, she ran into the locker room all the while dreading the appearance of the wicked woman. She stuffed her street clothes into her backpack and called her mom to come get her, but her mother was in a meeting and couldn't come until her regular pickup time. She called Horf hoping that he wasn't at work.

Ten minutes later, Tricia was never so glad to see a banged-up Nissan Sentra in her life. She climbed into the passenger seat and dumped her backpack on the floorboard in front of her.

"You going to tell me what's going on?" Horf asked her.

"What do you mean?"

"You're the only one out here."

She told him what had happened at practice and the lingering effects of the *hangakira*. "Why do you think I keep seeing this scary Asian woman?"

"No idea. I thought you said it just made the food taste bad. You never said the pills made you hallucinate like that. "

"I lost weight. That was all that mattered. And it's never been so vivid until now..." Her eyes filled with tears. "What if the stuff in the pills has accumulated in my body and is there for the rest of my life?"

"I'm sure your liver or whatever will deal with it, but until then, you've got to eat or you're going to be in real trouble." He reached into his backpack and took out his lunchbox. "Here. Have an apple I didn't eat. See what happens."

He handed her the lunchbox.

She opened it. The apple didn't leap out at her and go for her throat. That was a good thing. Determined to do something about her need for nourishment, she gritted her teeth and took a small shallow bite. The rubbery fruit chewed like a hunk of peeled skin pulled from a blister and tasted like an onion. She held her nose, took another loathsome bite, chewed, and swallowed. In this way, she managed to eat the whole thing.

"Yikes, Tricia, you looked like you were swallowing a handful of jacks."

"That was tough, but at least I've got something on my stomach. Thanks."

"No scary Asians?"

She shook her head.

At the stoplight, Horf tucked his lunchbox into his backpack. "Maybe if we get you something to drink and you drink a bunch of it, it will flush your system. What do you think?"

Her phone buzzed. She held up a finger "hold that thought" and answered it.

"What's up, Tricia? It's Trey. I got your number from Brynn. I hope you don't mind."

"Uh, no, not at all."

"Listen, I know I said we could study together sometime, but I was wondering if you wanted to go out to dinner with me this Friday night. You like Chinese?"

"Love it," she replied glancing at Horf. She could tell he was trying to figure out who was on the phone with her.

"I thought we could go to Dragon Lee's. You ever been there?"

"Nope, I haven't."

"It's super good. Moo goo gai pan, Kung Po chicken, egg drop soup, fortune cookies. It's all great. So, you in?"

Had she opened a fortune cookie that read she would be going on a dinner date with Trey Curtis this Friday, she would never have believed it. She just had to hope and pray that the remnants of those pills would be gone by then.

Oh, no!

Friday night!

The concert playing at the Elemental!

She had promised Horf she would go with him.

Damn.

Why couldn't anything ever be easy?

"Is something wrong?" Trey asked.

She rolled her eyes in frustration. "I forgot that I'm busy Friday night. Maybe next Saturday…"

Deadly Diet

"Oh," Trey said. She could hear the disappointment in his voice.

"He's just a friend," she added quickly. "I mean it's just a concert." She glanced at Horf who was clenching his jaw.

"That's not it," Trey said. "I'm going out of town Saturday with my folks. We're going upstate to visit my uncle."

She felt like somebody had punched her in the gut. She couldn't believe it. Her dream guy, the guy she thought would never notice her, had just asked her out and she couldn't go. The next words that came out of her mouth surprised her. "Listen, it's only Wednesday. I can ask Horf if he can get somebody else to go with him. He's right here."

"He won't care?"

"No, he won't mind," she said smiling at Horf who clearly seemed to mind.

"Okay, you know him better than I do. I'd be mad if a good-looking girl like you ghosted me. "

A good-looking girl like me! "He won't mind at all," she said.

Tricia turned to Horf knowing she had boxed him in.

It was a chilly ride the rest of the way home.

She spent the rest of the afternoon starving but avoiding a trip to the kitchen for fear of what she might encounter there.

As she sat on the bed in her room, she once more picked up her phone to call Horf but chickened out, not wanting to find out that she had done irreparable harm to their friendship with her selfish ask. It wasn't like her to diss a friend so harshly, but in this instance, going out with Trey meant more to her than just a regular date. It affirmed her acceptance at school. In her mind, she was no longer the fat girl from Florida who couldn't make the dance team, but a popular hottie who had turned the head of one of the best-looking guys at Bitterbrook High. So, what if Trey had treated her like a nonentity before her weight loss? At that time, she had been a bloated nothing, a loser, and the only person who wanted to hang with her was another fat loser.

As soon as that vile thought escaped from her pea brain, she wanted to crawl into a hole and bury herself in asphalt. What a Brynn she was becoming. Horf was the best guy, funny and caring. He wasn't a fat loser just because he didn't conform to what the majority of the kids at school expected. In fact, his individuality was what had drawn her to him in the first place. And besides that, he wasn't fat anymore. The other day, she had noticed how Horf was filling out with muscle. How he moved with more confidence and radiated good health. In a way, Tricia envied him because, unlike her, he had gotten into shape for himself not others, and did it in a methodical, natural, commonsense way, without resorting to some way-off-label pills that fudged up your senses even after you stopped taking them.

She glanced at the clock, dreading Mom's summoning to supper. Her face prickled at the thought of another bout of hallucinations confirming the damage she had done to her brain. If she didn't start eating soon, her body would rebel even more drastically than with the fatigue she'd been experiencing at dance practice. She knew from a report she had done last year about wartime prison camps that starvation could lead to, among other things, paranoia, cold skin, low blood pressure, and a condition known as lanugo, in which fine hair grows all over the body.

"That's all I need," she muttered. "From the Fat Lady at the circus to the Wolfwoman from Pago Pago."

The dreaded call to supper summoned her to the dining room table where dinner smelled like a burning funeral home. The charred stench was so intense it made her eyes water and she had to stumble away from the table. She hurried up the stairs to her room, jumped into the bed, and buried her face in the pillow. Were these pills never going to wear off?

Mom came into the bedroom. "Tricia, what's wrong?"

She rolled over and looked at her. "Nothing. I just feel a little queasy. I overdid it at practice today. Don't worry, I'll eat something a little later when I feel better."

Mom stared at her with pursed lips. "You're not still trying to lose weight, are you?"

"No, I swear. I just don't feel good at the moment." A dinner that smells like charred corpses always makes her a little nauseated.

"You want some Pepto?"

"I'll be all right. I'll just have something later."

Deadly Diet

Mom measured her with her eyes, gauging her truthfulness. She nodded. "Make sure you do."

She kissed her forehead and returned to the dining room table, leaving her to ponder the aftereffects of the pills.

A soft laugh sounded so close Tricia jolted. She turned and saw a movement to her left. She turned again and caught a hint of a shadow slinking to the right. Once more, out of the corner of her left eye, she glimpsed something moving. She whirled and saw the tail of a billowing silk kimono. She heard the giggle again.

She didn't wait to see or hear anything else. She jumped out of bed, bounded down the stairs, and ran into the living room. She turned on the television to get her mind off the visions brought on by her polluted mind. Was her body ever going to flush the drug from her system? Fear tore fissures in her composure. Panic slithered out of the cracks. She took several deep breaths and succeeded in driving her hysteria back. She was an acid freak stuck in a bad trip. She wondered if she would ever eat normally again.

TWENTY

Tricia struggled through the rest of the week holding her nose and force feeding herself until Friday, when miraculously, the terrible sensory hallucinations brought on by Tomoko's pills suddenly vanished. She had lost another three pounds by then, so she now had the ironic task of putting on pounds to get her weight back up to where she wanted it to be. She savored a solid breakfast of whole wheat French toast, vegan sausage, and fruit. For lunch, she enjoyed a bean burrito, a big salad, and a glass of orange juice. For dinner with Trey, she anticipated relishing a plate of something loaded with ginger, her favorite Chinese ingredient, while at the same time, overjoyed that she would be able to relish it without worry.

She glanced at the clock and saw that she had a half hour to finish getting ready for her date. She tightened her belt to the final hole in the strap and still could've used another one. The new jeans she'd bought on Monday were already loose around her butt. She noticed that her bra was also loose. She put on an old one that was a size smaller. She slipped into her favorite blouse, buttoned it, and found it to be a little too large as well.

"The incredible shrinking girl," she said.

She turned on the radio and the first thing she heard was an announcement about the concert at the Elemental that night. A sharp-edged blade of guilt nicked her. Since she'd broken their date, Horf had treated her the same as always. She wouldn't have blamed him if he kicked their friendship to the curb after she'd been such a bitch brushing him off like that. The funny thing was, when he told her that he was going to the concert with Danielle Marston, a friend of his sister Holly, Tricia had felt more than a little jealous.

Trey arrived at the Hall house around seven-thirty. Tricia cringed while Penny and her doll gave him the third-degree about whether or not he was Tricia's boyfriend. His answer that he would like to be brought a smile to Tricia's face.

A sculptured white dragon of marble greeted them at the entryway of Dragon Lee's. Intricate carved scales covered its muscular body. Stone fire flared from its toothsome jaws. The stone beast lurked amidst luscious plants with broad green leaves, a predator stalking in the jungle of some East Asian country. Its eyes seemed chillingly real and glared at them with feral intensity.

As they passed the statue, the leaves of one of the plants stirred. Tricia turned and looked. She didn't see anyone but imagined someone crouching behind the dragon, watching her.

"Coming?" Trey said, holding the door open for her.

She felt the rush of warm air coming from inside the restaurant and turned. "Oh, I'm sorry. I thought someone was…" Tricia saw the bemused expression on his face. "Never mind."

The host, a short Chinese woman with jet black hair and a polite smile, led them to their table. She wore an exquisite emerald kimono with a silky red dragon embroidered on the back.

She asked. "This table is okay?"

Trey nodded. "Can we get some menus?"

"Your waitress will be with you in a moment," the host said maintaining her smile. She returned to the foyer of the restaurant to greet customers.

"This is really nice," Tricia said, admiring the island of flowers and running waterfall that was the centerpiece of the room.

"Yeah. Smells great in here, too," Trey replied, looking around him. "Where is that server? I'm starving."

She took a hesitant whiff. She was relieved to smell nothing but the savory aroma of Chinese food.

As a menu magically appeared in front of her, a woman with a soft, measured voice said, "My name is Betty. I will be serving you this evening."

"About time," Trey said, under his breath.

Tricia took the menu and thanked her. The server gave a menu to Trey.

"Thanks, Betty," he said with a smirk.

She nodded and left to wait on the people at another table.

Trey floated his napkin into his lap. "All the Chinese chicks that work here have American names. Funny, but pretty smart business, am I right? I mean it's so hard to say those weirdo foreign names."

"Uh, yeah, I guess." Tricia perused the menu, chocking up his rude behavior to first date nerves.

"I hope you're starving, because the portions are mega," Trey said.

"Pretty hungry," she said demurely. She just hoped that she could resist licking the plate. "What are you gonna have?"

"I always have the same thing, the Emperor's Delight. If you like fish, it's the best thing on the menu, even though it's a little bizarre."

"What do you mean?"

"They leave the head on the trout."

"Lovely," she said. "Your dinner can watch you eat it."

"No, it's dead," Trey said. She didn't think he was kidding. He asked her what she was going to have.

"I was thinking of having the ginger vegetables with fried rice."

"Brack. Not a fan. I'm telling you, Tricia, you can't go wrong with the Emperor's Delight."

Deadly Diet

She smiled wondering if she had made a colossal mistake. Betty returned to their table. "Are you ready to order?" she asked, pencil poised to write.

They nodded and did so.

Tricia and Trey chatted about school for a few minutes before the conversation degenerated into a Treyfest. All he talked about was himself: his wins on the swim team, his good grades, his relationships with all the "babes" at school. She surprised herself when she felt uncomfortable to be amongst their number. Her contributions to the conversation were mostly grunts and nods. Whenever she tried to add anything, he barely acknowledged the comment before going back to what he had been saying about his favorite subject, himself. Once she tried to kid him about his hair being slightly green from too much chlorine and he responded with awkward silence.

Her thoughts turned toward Horf White. The anti-Trey. Even when he was overweight, Horf liked himself, but not in the narcissistic way that Trey did. Horf's manner was self-assured, without the need for braggadocio. And Horf listened to what she had to say intently and with genuine interest, even when she was blabbing about girly stuff or her clueless political views. On the other side of the interested spectrum, Trey didn't seem to give two sheets about anything she had to say. He just blathered on about himself while her mind wandered to the concert with Horf that she was missing. She was relieved when Betty brought out the sizzling, steaming plates that forced Trey to stuff his mouth with food.

As the raven-haired server placed their dishes in front of them, Tricia felt as if someone had just draped a blanket of ice over her. She looked up and noticed she was sitting under an air conditioning vent. She was relieved for a moment, until she remembered she wasn't in Florida anymore. It was winter in New York. She heard a raspy giggle behind her. Her stomach quivered. Just someone enjoying a joke, she told herself. Nothing to be worried about. She inhaled the aroma of her dinner. It smelled wonderful. Behind her, she heard the laughter again.

That couldn't be what she thought it was. Tricia had eaten breakfast and lunch that day. The aftereffects of the pills had left her. The pills couldn't be responsible.

The steaming ginger vegetables turned her stomach.

The giggle, a grating, hateful sound, crept into her ears again.

"This stuff is dank," Trey said. "I can't wait to dig in." He took his fork and stabbed the fish which flopped its tail on the plate. With his knife, he cut off a piece. The section from where he had sliced the flesh spurted blood. It hit the hot metal plate, steamed, and clotted.

"No," Tricia mouthed, horrified by the sight of the bleeding fish.

"Oh sorry," Trey said. "Are you one of those old-fashioned snacks who thinks a guy should wait until she takes her first bite?" He stuck another piece of gore into his mouth. "Not this guy. Mm, this is so good." A drop of blood slid from the corner of his mouth and spilled onto his shirt.

She gasped.

Trey stabbed the flopping fish with his fork and sliced away another flap of flesh. Blood spouted. The slapping trout splashed the gore onto the white tablecloth. Trey smiled and took another bite.

"Want to try some?" he said, cutting off a piece and holding the bloody chunk on his fork for her to sample.

"No, thank you," she said, desperately trying to gain control of her senses. "I—I'm not crazy about fish."

"How's your ginger whatever vegetables?"

"I—I'm waiting for it to cool."

"It should be okay. Mine's fine."

She worked up a smile and picked up her fork.

The trout on Trey's plate rolled an opaque eye in its socket to stare at her. The fish flapped and splashed clotted blood all over her. Tricia closed her eyes and told herself this was not happening.

She opened her eyes. Her platter boiled with fly larvae, squirming in a chunky brown sauce that smelled like a sewage plant on a sweltering summer day. The sound of the chewing maggots made her gag.

"What's wrong?" Trey asked.

Deadly Diet

The maggots tumbled over the edge of the plate and crawled toward her. "Get them away!"

"Tricia, everybody's looking," Trey said. He looked at the people around him and propped a dumb apologetic smile on his blood-splattered face.

The maggots falling off the plate exposed a massive grub that squirmed in the middle of the rice.

"Stop!" Tricia screamed.

"What the hell is wrong with you?" Trey demanded.

The bulky grub slipped out from the pile and wiggled toward her. It had a mouth full of tiny sharp teeth. She picked up her glass and crushed it. Green and yellow goo gushed from its sides. She lost control and projectile-vomited all over Trey.

"Damn, shit," Trey cried. He looked around the room, waving his arms. "It's okay, everybody, she's just sick."

Trey got up and took her arm. "Come on. You need to go to the bathroom."

Tricia looked down at his blood-soaked fingers on her wrist. She yanked her hand away from him. The fish on his plate smiled grotesquely. The squirming maggots crawled off the table and landed in her lap. She could hear them chewing. She screamed and jumped up from the table, slapping her thighs.

"Tricia, what are you high? You're making a damned idiot out of yourself..."

"Shut the hell up!" She shouted at the munching maggots.

Trey looked around the room again and smiled with that stupid apologetic grin. He tried to take her arm again.

"Get off me!" she screamed, brushing away the sickening little worms.

The concerned host arrived at the table. "What is wrong?"

"I dunno. She's flipping out," Trey said.

"Come, miss, we go outside."

Tricia stared at the woman's face covered in red-rimmed boils. She clamped her palm over her mouth as the boils erupted, spewing egg drop soup. She staggered away from her.

"Please, outside," the host said.

Trey grabbed Tricia's arm.

She pulled away.

The host stepped forward, spurting viscous yellow soup from her face.

"Get away!" Tricia screamed.

"I going to call the police if you do not leave," the host said. A huge boil jutted from her skin and a bulky maggot wriggled out from it.

Tricia shrieked.

"I'm outta here," Trey said, dropping two twenties and a ten on the table. "She's your problem now, this turnt-assed weirdo. Bye, Felicia."

"Wait a moment," the host said, snatching up the money.

"I'm gone," he said.

The strange chill drained from Tricia's body. She closed her eyes to try to control the swirling dizziness inside her head. When she opened them, her Asian nightmare was staring at her with that wicked grin on her face. She started to fall.

Strong fingers wrapped around her upper arms. She started to move. The next thing she knew she was standing in the parking lot outside the restaurant.

"Next time, you do your drugs, do someplace else," a Chinese man in a chef's hat shouted at her, before disappearing behind the red doors of the entrance.

As Tricia shambled to the curb and sat, the bitter taste of vomit and shame lingered in her mouth. Her stomach was still queasy. It was as though she had just gotten off a particularly vicious carnival ride. She looked around the parking lot, hoping to see Trey's car on the off chance he had changed his mind about leaving.

He hadn't.

Faint laughter rippled from the direction of the entryway. She turned toward the sound and saw the malevolent Asian woman. She shimmered and faded like a watercolor painting dropped in a fountain.

Tricia's face flushed with terror, and she feared that she might throw up again. She squeezed her eyes tightly shut, hoping the pain from the pressure she was creating would clear her head. Obviously, the hallucinations had returned, but she couldn't understand how they could be more vivid now than when she was actually taking the pills. It didn't make sense.

She decided to table those concerns for later. For now, she had to get a ride home. Her parents and Penny were visiting the Alberts tonight, but she wouldn't have called them anyway. Not when she had to explain what happened at the restaurant, and that meant lying like a psychopath to explain why she had screwed up her date with Bitterbrook High's best-looking boy. She looked at her phone and saw that it was just past eight. The concert at the club didn't start until nine. Maybe if she hurried, she could catch Horf before he left home for the Elemental.

She dialed his number and was relieved when she heard his voice come on the line.

"Horf, I need your help," she blurted.

"I thought you were out on a date with Trey."

"It didn't work out. Can you, and I know this is a BS ask, but can you please pick me up at the Chinese place?"

"Wait a sec, what do you mean, it didn't work out?"

"We went out to eat and things went bad."

"You're not making any sense. Where's Trey?"

"He left me at the restaurant."

"What?"

Her voice cracked. "I - I'm in trouble."

"What's wrong?"

"It started again. When the server brought our food, Trey's fish came to life. I saw maggots moving on my plate. Blood spurting. Whatever was in those pills is still messing with my brain." She choked off a sob.

"And Trey just left you there? That asshole."

"I don't blame him for leaving. I was screaming and acting all crazy."

"Well, I do," Horf said angrily. "What restaurant are you at?"

"Dragon Lee's."

"I'll be there in ten minutes. Wait out front."

A surge of guilt slammed her. "No, Horf, forget it. You'll be late for your concert. You know, the one I ditched to go out with Trey. I can walk. I deserve to walk."

"Just stay there and wait for me."

A lump came to her throat, blocking her words of gratitude. She nodded.

"You there?" Horf said.

Tricia swallowed and found her voice. "Yes, I just… Thank you, Horf. Thanks for coming." She waited at the curb, hoping she wouldn't experience any more visions.

Ten minutes squirmed past before Horf's car pulled into the parking lot. She ran over to the Sentra and jumped into the vehicle.

"Are you okay?" he asked.

"Better," she smiled. "If you hurry and take me home, you can still make the concert."

"I gave my ticket to my sister."

"What'd you do that for?"

"You sounded like you were in trouble," he said. "Besides, Holly wanted to go with Danielle, and they get along better than Danielle and I do."

"You're a great friend, you know that?" Tricia said. "I burnt you to go out with Trey, he leaves me in trouble, and you blow off a concert by two of your favorite bands to come help me."

"Yeah, I'm a saint," Horf said. "So, fill me in."

She took a deep breath and recounted the evening's events.

Horf thought for a moment and then said, "Do you still have some of those pills? I'm going to take a couple to Jack, at work. He's a pharmacist. He can send them off to a lab that can analyze them. Then we'll know for sure what's in them."

"I don't know if I want to know. Magic mushrooms or something. Aren't they decriminalized in Oregon?"

"Yeah, but I doubt shrooms would make you see scary Japanese ghost ladies and bloody fish and eyeballs that grow out of piles of maggots. At least, that's not what my older brother and his friends experienced. It must be something else."

"Okay. Let's find out what is in them. I have to know."

"Come on. I'll take you home and we can talk."

Tricia leaned over and kissed Horf—on the cheek. "Thank you," she said softly.

Horf turned to her, and their eyes met. In the light of that lone streetlamp, she saw him in an entirely new way. He was no longer the pudgy sidekick who tickled her funny bone; he was her knight in shining armor who came to rescue her. For the first time, she realized how attractive he was, and it had nothing to do with him losing weight.

"Don't worry, Tricia," he said, putting a warm palm against her cheek. "In a week or so, we'll find out what's in the pills and go from there."

TWENTY-ONE

Ginseng?" Tricia cried, staring at the results of the chemical analysis that Horf had just handed her. Since they sent the pills off to the chemists, she had lost six more pounds in seven days. A week of chills and the most appalling food: peaches filled with rotted meat, bread teeming with weevils, macaroni slugs and snot cheese. And watching over her suffering like a vulture waiting for its dinner to die was the gaunt Asian woman, getting younger and more frightening each day. School was a disaster. Her concentration was gnat-like. Her grades were abysmal. And to top it off, on the eve of the first appearance of the Ravenettes, Coach Mustache Milton let her go from the team. Her dismissal and the disastrous date with Trey had turned Brynn and her squad against her. They had taken to calling her Trippy Tricia, implying that drug abuse was her problem. Guess saving someone's life didn't have the cachet it once did.

Deadly Diet

And now, to put a putrid cherry on top of the worst week of her life, Horf was telling her that the pills were nothing more than ginseng tablets.

"But the hallucinations—how do they explain them?" She cried.

"They can't. Jack suggests you see a doctor that specializes in eating disorders."

"That's what my mom wants me to do. She set up an appointment for me this afternoon at some 'world-renowned' health clinic that deals with eating disorders. EADIS, it's called, short for eating disorders. To her, I have all the warning signs of anorexia—intolerance of cold, skipping meals and making excuses, not eating much food, concentration issues. Not to mention losing a shit ton of weight. "

"She's right. Someone professional needs to check you out. They can give you an IV full of stuff to put some weight on you. You're starting to look sick skinny."

"Don't you think I know that? It's not like I don't want to eat right or think I'm too fat or I'm sticking my fingers down my throat. I just can't eat when my red beans and rice have a skinned live rat in them. I can tell you one thing. If the doctors can't help me, I know somebody who can."

"Who's that?"

"Tomoko Tanaka. I've been thinking about her a lot. When I first met her, she was always looking over her shoulder as if someone were watching her. And there was that time in the cafeteria when she couldn't stand to be in there. I bet the pills messed up her head, too."

"That doesn't make sense. The pills are just ginseng, remember? Ginseng doesn't cause hallucinations."

"So why give them to me? That's what doesn't make any sense." She ran her fingers through her lifeless hair and sighed in frustration. "Tomoko was evasive when I first asked her about the side effects of the pills. She seemed angry that I was questioning their effectiveness, and since they worked, I didn't pursue it."

"Because you were losing weight fast."

"Exactly," Tricia said. "Then she left to be with her grandfather in Old Town and things got worse for me. I tried calling her, but she never returned my calls."

"Sounds fishy."

"Don't remind me of my date with Trey," she said, trying to lighten the moment.

"I mean it sounds maggoty."

She laughed. Gallows humor they call it. "I never told you this, but she did something else that was weird when she gave me the pills."

"What's that?"

"Before she gave them to me, she made me read from this parchment. You know what they used before paper, made from animal skins"

"She made you read what from this parchment?"

"These Japanese words. She said it was to summon the *hangakira*, the spirit warrior." I got the pouch from the dresser and showed him the parchment.

"That's mondo weird. How could reading Japanese have anything to do with what's happening to you?"

"I don't know, but I'm going to find out." Tricia stuffed the parchment into her pocket. "Holly gave me Tomoko's address. Tomorrow, I'm going to see her."

"We're going to see her," Horf said.

"Okay, we're going. And when we get there, we're going to get some answers."

She looked at the clock on the wall. "Mom's taking me to that clinic in fifteen minutes. I guess I better get ready."

"Okay, I'm outta here then," Horf said, grabbing his jacket off her hope chest. As he walked toward the bedroom door, he slipped it on.

She put on her sweater. "I'll walk you out to your car."

Dark clouds, the harbinger of a storm, blotted out the sun. A chilly wind whipped the trees in the front yard. She crossed her arms and shivered. "Great, just what we need. Another wonderful day of Portlandian rain to make me even more miserable."

"Look at it this way," Horf said. "You won't be thinking about drinking any milk shakes with ground cow udders in them."

"That's a comforting thought." She put her hand on Horf's shoulder. "You can always drag a smile out of me, you know that?"

"Smile dragging is a lost art," Horf said.

She looked toward the house. "I better get back inside and get ready to go to the clinic. Mom should be here any minute. She had to drop Penny off at Mrs. Alquist's."

Horf unlocked his car door and got in. "Call me when you get home, and we'll make plans for tomorrow."

Tricia stared at him for an uncomfortably long moment.

"What? Do I have a booger?"

She smiled. "You're a great guy, you know that?"

"A great friend, you mean."

She leaned into the car and kissed him on the lips. "I mean a great guy."

He seemed a little gobsmacked by the impromptu kiss. He rolled up the window and started the engine, his face a blend of shock and delight. He put the car in reverse and started to pull out of the driveway. He stopped the car with a slight squeal. He rolled down his window and stuck his head out. "You're great, too." He blew her a kiss and drove off. Tricia skipped into the house, feeling better than she had in weeks.

She dressed and waited in the living room for her mom to pull into the driveway and park the car. She beeped the horn.

She locked the door and hustled to the car. She opened the door to climb into the passenger seat but froze when she saw the gaunt specter of the Asian woman floating in the back seat, watching her. She choked back a scream and backed away from the car.

"Tricia, what's the matter?" Mom said.

The specter covered her mouth with a bony hand, giggled and then slowly faded into her reflection in the window. The familiar chill came over Tricia.

"What's wrong?" Mom said. She held a half-eaten pear in her hand. The fruit teemed with ants. She took a sip of bottled water filled with sludge.

"Answer me." Her mother dropped the pear into her car's mini trash can.

Tricia closed her eyes and slumped into the passenger seat. "Nothing's the matter," she croaked, the insides of her cheeks were sticking to her teeth. She looked at her bottle of water. It was clear. She picked it up and drank some before it changed back to muck. "Can we just go?"

"Of course," Mom said. "You sure you're okay, honey?" She put the car in reverse.

"I'm fine. Let's get this over with."

TWENTY-TWO

Forty-five minutes later, they pulled into the parking lot of the EADIS Clinic located on Sauvie Island on the Columbia River. The clinic was a three-story rectangular building with gray stucco walls and bay windows that afforded each room with a view of the grounds. The building stood nestled in a stand of Douglas firs. Under the trees, concrete park benches sat empty. The only sign of life was a huge bundle of raingear that was no doubt a resident of the clinic waddling down a nature trail.

Mom popped the trunk and got out of the car. Tricia did the same and scalpels of cold wet air sliced through her clothes, cutting to the bone. Since she had lost weight, her resistance to the cold sucked and was getting worse with each pound she dropped. She pulled her jacket tight and huddled next to her mother.

"Isn't this a pretty place?" she said, tugging a suitcase out of the trunk.

"Wait! I'm staying here?"

"Maybe. They told me to pack for a week. In case, they make that determination." She slammed the trunk.

"Mom, I can't stay here for a week."

"We'll see what they say."

"Just leave it in the trunk. You're gonna curse me bringing it in there."

"Curse you?" she said shaking her head. "That's silly." Suitcase in hand, she led Tricia down a cobblestone sidewalk toward the main entrance of the facility.

The toasty temperature of the reception area thawed them. The pictures of smiling healthy-looking girls that lined the wall warmed her mother's heart. Success stories. Tricia and her mother sat on a buttery-soft leather couch and waited for them to call her for her appointment. Tricia took off her jacket and scooped up a magazine, but before she had a chance to begin reading, a smiling woman in a blazer came out to greet them. Her name tag read Naomi. "Tricia, can you please give your mother your phone?"

"My phone?"

"No distractions. No triggers. EADIS policy."

She huffed and handed Mom her phone.

Naomi gave her a document on a clipboard. "We need you to fill out this questionnaire. Your answers will help us determine your disorder."

"But I don't have a disorder. I want to eat."

"Then why don't you, honey?" Mom asked plaintively. "Your dinner's always untouched."

"Mom, I try, but I can't."

"Tricia, you keep saying that."

The woman reached out and took her mother's arm. She spoke gently. "For now, why don't we have Tricia fill out the questionnaire? You can come with me, and I'll show you our facilities while Tricia works here."

Mom nodded. "We'll be back in a little while, honey." She followed Naomi out of the waiting room.

Tricia filled out the questionnaire. Suddenly, she felt a presence observing her. She looked around to see who was there, and when she

138

did, she saw her phantom advancing toward her. She appeared much younger now. Closer to twenty. Her arms outstretched as if to embrace Tricia. She tumbled out of the chair. The spirit smiled grotesquely, revealing her blackened teeth.

"What are you?" Tricia whispered.

The repulsive grin widened and then, without provocation, howled and soared toward her. As she hit her, Tricia screamed and reeled onto the table, knocking over the lamp. When she recovered, she caught her own reflection in the glass of the bookcase. A bony hand protruding from her shoulder withdrew into her body.

"She's inside me!" Tricia cried.

The familiar icy chill spread over her. The terrifying, unbelievable notion that this creature's invasion of her body was what was causing her visions made her head swim. The room matched her beating heart, expanding and contracting. The pictures of the smiling girls on the wall mocked her. Her knees weakened and her legs crumpled.

As she collapsed to the floor, she saw three pairs of atrociously distorted legs stalking toward her. She heard people talking, a soothing baritone, a woman's gentle voice, her mother's concerned cry. They were all speaking at once, and their words made no sense, babbling incoherencies that infuriated and confused her. Nonsense. Tricia caught the words "needs to eat."

She giggled, but it was not her laughter that she heard. It was the rasping cackle of the woman inside her.

Tricia tried to scream, but her world winked off.

When she regained consciousness, she was sitting with Trey Curtis at Dragon Lee's restaurant. The server had just taken the main course orders.

"So, how do you like being on the dance team?" Trey asked her.

"Fine," she said, dosed with déjà vu.

"How do you like the spring roll?" She looked down at her plate and saw a half-eaten appetizer. It smelled wonderful. She picked it up and took a small bite. It tasted better than it smelled.

What was going on?

Their server Betty passed them carrying an aromatic ginger-flavored dish that made Tricia's mouth water. "Your meal is coming next."

"I hope you're hungry, because the portions are huge," Trey said.

"Starving," she replied.

The conversation continued until Betty put her food in front of her and removed the cover of her dish. Tricia could not speak. She gagged and turned away from the dish that sat on the plate in front of her. It was the charred head of Horf White, baked in a scream.

A hand shot out of Horf's mouth. Fingers wrapped around her throat. Tricia stood, backing away from the table, pulling the hand with her and hauling the Asian woman out of her friend's mouth in a grotesque version of birth.

She snapped awake. She could not breathe. She sat up in an unfamiliar bed and gasped for air. Her lungs pulled oxygen into their starving chambers. A grateful shudder shivered through her. Tricia had an IV attached to a bag of clear liquid dripping into her arm. She wore a hospital gown.

A polished cherrywood bookcase anchored the room in which she found herself. YA books of all genres lined the shelves. A reading lamp rested on top of a small cherrywood table that separated two brown leather chairs. Mom was sitting in one of them.

"I'm glad to see you're awake," she said. "How are you feeling?"

"I'm cold. Oh my God, I'm still so fricking cold."

"Get under the blankets."

"You don't understand, Mom."

Her mother got up from the chair and sat next to her on the bed. "Dr. Parsons told me to get him when you woke up, so he can explain to you what's going to happen during your stay here at the clinic. Be back in a sec."

"I can't stay here, damn it."

"Tricia, you need help."

"I swear I don't have any eating disorder. I do not have anorexia or bulimia or anything like that."

"Honey, we've been over this before."

"I know, but I never told you why I can't eat. What I did."

140

Deadly Diet

Mom put her palm against her cheek. "So, tell me."

"Get my jeans over there." They were draped over a coat hanger. She did.

Tricia tugged the parchment out of the pocket and handed it to her. "And this is what?"

She explained the whole story, from the first meeting with Tomoko to the last episode of what she described as demonic possession.

Mom stared at her. Her pitiful, patronizing smile was all Tricia needed to see to know that she didn't believe her.

"Oh my God," she cried. "You're going to be like one of the mothers in the movies who doesn't believe her kid when she tells her a monster's trying to kill her?"

"It's just – you're possessed like the girl in *The Exorcist*? It's pretty hard to wrap my head around that."

"Get me out of here and we'll go to Old Town to find Tomoko and I'll prove it to you. Holly Henderson gave me her address. I just…" She stiffened when she felt warm again.

"Tricia, what's wrong?"

The demonic Asian sat next to her mother. She smiled at her.

"What's the matter?" Mom asked.

The malevolent woman melted into her mother's body.

"No!" Tricia shouted.

Mom's face went blank. The translucent image of the demon lurked behind her mother's features. She wobbled to her feet and smiled jerkily. When the grin finally settled onto her face, it looked like the frozen smile of a mannequin. Mom turned and ran as fast as she could, slamming into the third story window. She bounced off, leaving behind a large crack. Her head lolled toward her. A trail of blood leaked from her crushed nose. She flashed a plastic smile.

"Mom!"

She ran and slammed herself into the window again, shattering the glass. She staggered backward and gathered her balance. Blood poured from her clean-sliced skin, coating her arms, painting her blank face crimson. She looked out of the window again and Tricia knew what she was going to do. She yanked the needle out of her arm, spraying blood and glucose all over the sheet and tried to stop her mother from hurling herself into the splintered glass. She pulled out of her feeble grasp and sprinted into the weakened window. It gave way and she plunged three stories onto the pavement below.

"Oh my God! Oh my God! Mom! Somebody, help!" She picked up the remote and stabbed the call button to summon the nurse.

No one answered.

She staggered to the window and saw her mother lying unmoving on the sidewalk. An expanding pool of blood framed her head. The demon shot from her mother's body and soared toward her. Its entry into Tricia's body was so sudden the icy chill stung her. She fought the demon for control of her mind so she could summon help.

Tricia ran for the door and fell out into the hallway crashing into an orderly carrying a tray of food. A hairnet held his black dreadlocks. "Where you going, Missy?" the orderly asked.

She looked down at the plate and saw steaming heaps of intestines clumped on top of a twitching peeled dog. The orderly scooped a handful of ropes of foul flesh and offered them to her.

She screamed and slapped the tray out of his hands. She tried to tell him about her mother, but frosty fingers choked off her words. She couldn't breathe. Her face started to pulsate to the beat of her wildly pounding heart. The pressure in her chest made her feel as if she was going to burst.

"Oh, my God, Dr. Parsons, she's turning blue!"

Hands appeared all around her.

Holding her down.

She gulped the air.

"Tricia, it's going to be all right."

"Dr. Parsons, she's bleeding."

"Put pressure on her arm."

"Look at her face. What's she doing?"

"Don't let her swallow it!"

Fingers grasped her tongue.

"Benjamin, help me here."

"Tricia! Oh no, please, honey, don't die."

"We need you to stay calm."

Deadly Diet

Demonic laughter.

Madness.

From the edges of her sanity, Tricia could tell they were lifting and carrying her back into her room. Voices drifted in and out of her awareness.

An injection of oblivion brought relief. Part of her hoped she would never wake up again. The other part of her knew what she had to do if she wanted to stay alive. She had to get out of the clinic and find Tomoko Tanaka. If she didn't, the demon would surely starve her to death.

When Tricia awakened, it was six o'clock in the evening. She looked out the unbroken window at the pouring rain, stunned. Had she been out long enough for them to replace the window or was she in a different room? And what about her mom? Was she okay? She pressed the call button for the nurse. She appeared at the door. "What can I get you, hon?"

"How's my mom?"

"She's home."

"Home? Is she alright?"

She looked confused. "I believe so. We can check in the morning. We don't need you getting upset again."

Her beeper buzzed. "Duty calls."

Tricia waited a moment, and then carefully pulled the IV out of her arm. She pressed the sheet against the wound until she was sure it had stopped bleeding.

She threw on her clothes, checked for the nurse, and then hustled down the hall. There was a landline phone at her station. She picked up the handset to call Horf when she realized that his number was in her phone. She closed her eyes and tried to picture the number and then it hit her. *You're not thinking right, Tricia. If the demon could possess your mother and make her hurt herself, then it could possess Horf and make him do the same.*

She would have to make the trip alone.

She saw a purse on the desk. Inside was a key ring with keys and a fob for a Kia. She tugged the key ring out of the purse and took off for the front door.

As she hustled through the waiting room, Tricia heard the nurse calling her name. She ignored her and picked up her pace. She slammed through the double doors of the entrance and ran through the chilly rain to the lone Kia Optima in the lot. She pressed unlock on the fob and heard the locks pop. She jumped into the car and started the engine.

A hand rapped urgently on the driver's side window. A face appeared.

"What do you think you're doing?" The nurse shouted. "Tricia, open this door immediately!"

Tricia slammed the car into Drive and pressed the gas pedal. The nurse banged on the window.

"Stop, Tricia! Everything's going to be okay," she cried.

Tricia ignored her. She pulled away slowly until she was sure that the nurse was clear of the vehicle before she punched it and sped out of the parking lot. She would worry about the theft charges later.

When she reached a stop sign, she paused to tell Tomoko's address to the car's GPS system. It calculated the route, and she was on her way in her stolen car.

TWENTY-THREE

By the time Tricia made the drive from the clinic to the section of Portland known as Old Town, it was close to seven o'clock. Traffic was bumper to bumper because of an accident that blocked one lane. A lengthy line of cars snaked through the streets, winking red and yellow every time a car from one side or the other was allowed to pass the crash site. Tricia was dragging eyelids. Every time the voice of the GPS piped up to tell her the next direction to take, she jolted jitters from the adrenaline dump. Her nerves were a tightrope upon which her composure teetered. A big black Cadillac Escalade cut in front of her, causing her to slam on the brakes and almost shed her skin. She cursed the driver and shakily waited for the traffic to clear.

It took another half hour to get to Tomoko's apartment building. It was a giant square of bricks called ironically The Gardens. Tricia got lucky when a car pulled out of a parking space across the street. She whipped into it and parked. Out of habit, she reached for her phone to text Tomoko to announce her arrival but failed having forgotten the clinic had confiscated it.

145

She crossed the street and headed up the sidewalk. A crew of sketchy teenagers, drinking beer and smoking weed, huddled on an apartment stoop. She kept her eyes straight ahead of her and confidently marched past them, her insides churning from the potential threat of confrontation. One of them said, "Hi." The others watched her pass without comment. So much for stereotypes.

She arrived at the Gardens. She tried to open the door. Locked. *What did you expect, a welcome mat and an "I Heart Burglars" sticker?* She sat on the stoop and pondered her next move.

The deadbolt lock popped from the inside. She jumped to her feet. The door opened and a woman, fishing through her purse, exited. Tricia caught the door with her foot. She didn't notice.

She stepped inside a cramped hallway lit by a bare yellow bulb. She hustled to the elevator and pressed the button for the ninth floor. As she waited, a bony old Asian man in a checkered jacket and polyester pants entered the building and stood next to her. His dyed black hair needed degreasing. He smiled at her, his dentures a fierce white. She smiled back, ready to launch a knee into his groin should he try to touch her.

With his hands behind his back, the man rocked on his heels, whistling a bouncy tune Tricia didn't recognize. He glanced at her and smiled again.

She did the same, still prepped to fire a groin shot in the event he moved on her.

He started whistling again, only the tune was different. It was a haunting melody, pervaded with sorrow, with a definite Japanese vibe. Ominous rumblings boiled in Tricia's gut.

The man kept rocking, back and forth, whistling his melancholy tune.

She caught him out of the corner of her eye watching her as if anticipating her reaction to his sad Japanese tune. Her uneasiness toward him increased.

She turned to show him that she was aware of his scrutiny. He smiled knowingly as if they shared some awful secret between them.

She looked away.

Hurry up, elevator.

Deadly Diet

The tone of his incessant song twisted slowly, the mood shifting from mournful to ominous.

Come on. Hurry.

The tune perverted abruptly into a discordant jumble. It was as if the whistling man had changed into something terrible. She tried to relax her muscles so she could deliver the knee with as much force as possible.

Abruptly, the man stopped whistling.

Dead silence.

She held her breath.

The man stopped rocking and turned toward her.

This was it.

The elevator bell rang. The thin man got on and pressed the button. "Coming?" he said with a pleasant smile.

She shook her head and ran for the door to the stairs. She climbed nine flights in record time. She found the apartment and knocked until Tomoko cracked the door as far as the chain lock would allow. She stared at her, and tears came to her eyes.

"We need to talk," Tricia said bluntly.

Tomoko nodded and opened the door.

Tricia barely recognized the girl that stood before her. Her face was full, her eyes bright. The flesh on her arms was plump and smooth. She suddenly realized how terribly thin she had been on the day she had given her the pills.

She heard an old man speaking Japanese from a bedroom. Tomoko answered.

"Come, Tricia, let us go into my room."

She followed her.

Tomoko sat on her bed and hung her head. "I am sorry for what I have done to you, Tricia. I have committed a great act of deception for which I will be punished in the afterlife."

"Save the apology and tell me what's happening to me?" Tricia handed her the parchment. "Starting with this. Those pills you gave me are just ginseng."

"The pills are part of the deception."

147

"You keep saying deception. What deception?"

Tomoko raised her hand to quell her questions. "Please, sit, I will explain it all."

She dropped into an office chair in front of a small desk. "Go ahead."

"I once told you of Cho the girl at the retreat who gave me the pills. What I did not tell you was that an Oni possessed Cho."

"An Oni?"

"A demon."

Tricia felt outside herself, as if I were watching a horror movie in which I was the star.

Tomoko held up the parchment. "The last words you spoke to complete the ritual sealed the possession. *Takeda Katsu Hime, watashi no tamashī wa anata no monodesu.* In English it means, Princess Katsu Takeda, my soul is yours."

"So, I invited her to take possession of me. And this Katsu Takeda was a princess?"

"Of the Tokugawa Shogunate, a vain and cruel practitioner of the Dark Arts, and the centuries since her death have neither lessened her vanity nor her cruelty. Surely, you saw her blackened teeth and the powdered ink eyebrows of the noblewoman in Ancient Japan, relived visions of her cruelty when she first entered you, the whippings, the samurai who loved her committing seppuku."

Tricia remembered. "But what does she get out of this possession?"

"Fed."

"Fed on what?"

"You become a feast for demons. It is the nature of the Oni to feed off human misery. And what would cause greater pain than to have your wish granted, while at the same time that wish destroys your life? The grandmother of Cho had warned her granddaughter of the hunger of the Oni, but Cho was young and scoffed at such superstition. She believed it was the pills that were causing her visions and stopped taking them."

"But the hallucinations didn't stop, did they?"

Tomoko shook her head. "Cho chose not to accept what her grandmother said needed to be done to save herself, instead believing the psychiatrists at the eating disorder clinic could cure her through therapy and medication."

"But they couldn't, so she caved and put the curse on someone else."

"Like all others before her. Only she was too late. Her damaged organs shut down and she died, the kindness that delayed her decision killed her."

"How do you know all this about this Princess Katsu?"

"As I told you, Grandfather works as a curator for the Asian history museum. I asked him if he could research Takeda Katsu Hime. He found mention of her in a Japanese history of the Shogunate of the Tokugawa clan. It was only a paragraph, but it spoke of her cruelty and the belief amongst her enemies that she was *kitsune-tsukai*, a fox witch. In Japanese folklore, humans employed foxes to do their bidding because the fox is a powerful trickster, with powers of shape changing, possession, and illusion."

"Sounds about right for the craziest shit I have ever heard. And the curse?"

"Grandfather traced it to the book *Nihan no Majutsu*, Witchcraft of Japan. He said that it was a *daburu kurosu*, a curse that gives you the thing you want most, but makes you suffer for it until someone takes the curse upon them."

"But I saw this demon possess my mom and make her jump out a third story window."

"If you saw that, it was the Oni making you believe that your mother did herself harm. Imagine the feast of pain you fed to her when you believed your mother jumped through the window or worse was dead. This is why the demon must possess a being with a mind so that it can manipulate their emotions."

Tricia recalled the wrenching of her soul when she saw her mom crumpled on the sidewalk, her head leaking pools of blood, and envisioned the demon gorging upon her agony. The fingers on both her hands folded into fists. "So, how can I fight Katsu Hime?"

"You cannot. The only way to be free of the Oni is to die by your own hand, or you must trick another into accepting the demon inside her."

"Either I kill myself, or I curse someone else, those are my choices? How can I do that to someone knowing what will happen to them? How could you do that to me?"

Tomoko turned away from her. "When Katsu grows so strong that she torments you with no end in sight, you will do anything to stay alive and be free of her."

She grabbed Tomoko by the arms and shook her. "But why me?"

The Japanese girl met her anger with indignation. "You wanted to be thin at any price. You said so. Now, if you want to be rid of the Oni, you must find someone else to take your place."

"There must be another way!"

Tomoko held the parchment for Tricia to take back. "There is no other way."

TWENTY-FOUR

This is not happening; this is not happening, Tricia kept telling herself, horribly aware of the demon inside her. She had been driving for twenty minutes without incident when she felt the chill. Now, she was staring at a billboard from which a chocolate sundae had just exploded, sending a geyser of yellow-green pus into the air. The ooze splattered all over the windshield blocking her vision of the road. She panicked, slammed on the brakes, and pulled over into the emergency lane. She closed her eyes and fought the thing inside her. When she opened her eyes, the windshield was clear, but a hamburger with hairy spider legs crawled off the face of the billboard and scuttled toward her car. The halves of its buns were snapping like giant jaws. She threw the car into reverse, backing away from the eight-legged quarter-ton pounder.

"Not there. Not there. Not there," Tricia chanted, keeping the pedal to the metal while trying to avoid sliding into a ditch. A surge of fury cut through her terror. She slammed on the brakes and shouted, "You are not fricking there!"

151

The hamburger sprang into the air and vanished.

She dropped her forehead onto the steering wheel and rubbed her aching eyes. She had to get the hell home and get to bed. She pulled back onto the road and kept her gaze on the road, away from billboards, especially those advertising restaurants.

As fatigue settled into her bones, she felt antsy, wanting to straighten her aching legs. She also desperately wanted to shut her burning eyes, but knew if she did, she would be pasted to a tree faster than you can say highway fatality.

Hoping the cold would brace her, she turned off the heater and cracked the window. It worked for a little while, but when the cold penetrated her bones, her quivering muscles made it difficult to maintain control of the steering wheel. She had to turn the heat back on or risk trembling to the point where she swerved into an oncoming semi-truck.

The soothing warmth provided by the heater was, to borrow a phrase, a *daburu kurosu*, a blessing and a curse. The heat comforted her, while at the same time dragging her eyelids to half-mast. And then a realization snapped her awake: if she felt warm that meant the spirit wasn't inside her. She turned and faced the demon sitting in the seat next to her. Katsu Hime grinned, exposing her black teeth. Tricia lashed out with her fist and hit her. The demon spirit exploded into thousands of glowing particles. Slowly the particles stopped swirling and began to re-form into the princess.

"Leave me alone!" Tricia screamed slamming her fist into the spirit again, shattering her. She pressed the window button and cracked the passenger side window just enough to cause the stream of air to form a suction that dragged the phantom's fragments into the night.

She sighed with relief and pressed the gas pedal to the floor, hoping to outrun the ghost.

She had just pulled onto Sawmill Road when the blare of a siren snapped her attention toward the road. Blue and white lights pulsated frantically inside the car. In the rearview mirror she saw a highway patrol car barreling down the road behind her. Her first thought was that she was going to prison for a long time for grand theft auto.

Deadly Diet

She pulled over, careful not to drive to close to the edge of a drop-off into a deadfall of trees and waited for the trooper to pull in behind her.

As she watched the patrol car roar past her in a swirl of spinning light, she pumped her fist a little and checked for traffic in the rearview mirror. Katsu Hime sprang from the back seat and slid into her body. Tricia tried to kick her out.

She lost.

It was then she realized she had parked in front of a billboard for the Pancake Palace. Two runny yellow eyes stared at her. Between them was a pocked and leprous nose that could have been a biscuit. Two strips of flayed skin that had once been bacon formed lips that twisted into a smile. The loathsome head fell off the sign and rolled onto the hood of the car. It started bouncing up and down, pounding the metal. Had this been a movie, the sight of this ridiculous bouncing pancake creature would have struck her as funny… no… not funny… fricking hilarious. She would have pointed at the silly breakfast beast and screeched with hysterical laughter, "You hop, I hop, we all hop."

But this was no movie.

And laughs were screams.

Tricia started the car intending to drive it into the deadfall to end her terror. The demon sensed this. Katsu Hime poked her head out of her stomach, grinning that blackened smile, before fleeing Tricia's body and disappearing into the night.

The billboard and her body temperature returned to normal.

Tricia gathered herself. She slammed her hand against the steering wheel and shouted, "Why did you do this to me, Tomoko?"

As she put the car in gear and pulled out onto the deserted road, the sobering answer came to her, if she didn't find a way out of this someone else would have to start asking the same question about her.

TWENTY-FIVE

Tricia didn't know whether her parents were going to kiss her or kill her when she came staggering through the door. "Where the hell have you been?" Dad said. She could tell he was battling to control his temper. "You had us half-worried to death."

"I'm sorry. I couldn't stay there. I had something to do."

"So, you steal a nurse's car and tear out of the clinic!" He shouted, losing his battle. "You're lucky she decided not to press charges. I called as soon as I heard you pull up."

"You went into the city, didn't you?" Mom said. "To see that girl."

"I had to see her. I told you why."

"Tricia, your mom told me about what you think is happening to you."

"And you don't believe me anymore than she does."

"We want you to give the doctors a chance. You're just not thinking right."

Penny padded into the room. To Tricia's horror, her sister carried a couple of doughnuts and a glass of milk in her small hands.

Deadly Diet

"What are you doing up?" Mom said.

"Me and Suzy wanted a snack."

Tricia heard a whispered giggle behind her. She turned and saw the Oni floating toward her, her kimono flowing behind her.

"Penny, get out of here with that shit," she snapped.

"Tricia, there's no reason for that sort of language," Dad said.

"Take it away now!" She screamed.

Penny backed away from her, her eyes wide with fright. "Momsuds, tell her to stop yelling at me."

"Tricia, please stop, you're scaring all of us," Mom said.

Katsu Hime drifted toward Tricia, looking as if she wanted to take a bite out of her with those awful black teeth.

She bolted toward the stairs.

"Tricia, you stay here!" Dad yelled.

"God, Alan, she needs help," Mom said. "We have to get her back to EADIS."

"Penny, put those doughnuts back in the package, put the milk in the fridge and go back to bed. Tricia, you get back here right now."

She kept running for the sanctuary of her bedroom. She yanked open the door, slammed it, and locked it, knowing full well that it wouldn't keep out the demon. But it would keep out her mother and father, and Penny, with her doughnuts.

She could hear her parents coming up the stairs.

The doorknob rattled.

"Tricia, open this door," Mom demanded.

"I can't."

"Open the goddamn door now!" Dad yelled.

"Alan, please, stay calm. She's sick," Mom said. "Please open the door. We want to help you."

"You can't!" Tricia sobbed.

The Oni flowed through the door and floated to the ceiling to watch the spectacle.

"Open the door so we can talk, honey," Mom pleaded. "We're not mad at you for taking the pills. We want to help. You've starved your ioned# Vincent Courtney

brain and you're not thinking right. You know there's no such thing as demons and possessions. You have to know that."

"We're worried about you, Tricia. Dr. Parsons can help you get through this."

Tricia glanced up at the hovering grinning specter. "Nobody can help me," she cried.

"Of course, they can. You have an eating disorder."

"Yeah, *oni*rexia." She laughed wildly.

"Okay, honey," Mom said. "If you want to be alone right now, we understand that, but we're going to take you back to the clinic in the morning."

"And you are not going to change our minds," Dad added.

Their footsteps faded down the hallway. With her plate of misery empty, Katsu Hime faded as well.

Tricia jumped onto the bed and buried her face in her pillow. How could she have been so foolish as to come home knowing she sounded like a lunatic? What did she expect her parents to do but return her to the clinic?

She had to go somewhere to hideout, a place where there would be no food to terrify her, where she could think of another way to free herself from this curse. She couldn't trick someone else into saying the prayer that she held so lightly in her pocket and so heavily in her heart. A plan formulated in her mind.

She got up from the bed, unlocked the door, and padded to the master bedroom where Mom and Dad were getting ready for an early bedtime. Their worrying over her had worn them out. She stood in the doorway and said softly, "I'll go back to the clinic tomorrow. I'm sorry for all the trouble I've caused."

Her mother ran over and took her in her arms. "We just want you to get better, honey."

Her father hugged them. "The clinic can help you."

"I know. I just panicked today. Since I lost so much weight, my mind's been acting weird. I want to go back to the clinic."

Mom smiled with relief. "You're making the right decision."

"I hope so," Tricia said. "I love you guys."

Mom smiled and kissed her head. "We love you, too, honey."

156

"Yeah," Dad said, hugging her. "Now, get to bed and get some rest. You look exhausted."

"I am." Tricia smiled weakly, knowing that her night had yet to begin.

TWENTY-SIX

Tricia waited until her parents were asleep before she started to pack. She hated having to sneak out and upset them by becoming a runaway, but she just couldn't afford to go back to the EADIS Clinic if she wanted to survive the Oni. After stuffing her suitcase with clothes, she returned the parchment to the pouch, and put it into her bag as well. She didn't want anyone in her family to read the curse and inadvertently summon the demon. That is what she told herself, but deep in the primitive part of her lizard brain where survival lurked, she knew the real reason and hated herself for thinking it.

She snuck out of her room carrying the suitcase.

And there she stood in the dim glow from the nightlight in the hall.

Her night owl of a little sister rubbed her bleary eyes and then squinted at her. "Whatcha doin', Trisha Wisha?"

"Just putting my suitcase downstairs to get a head start on going to the clinic in the morning."

"Momsuds and Daddly say you're not feeling good, that's why you yelled at me."

"Yeah, I don't feel too good, and I'm sorry I yelled at you. I didn't mean it."

"You moving to the clinic?"

"Just for a little while."

"Suzy and me are gonna miss you."

Penny pressed the record button on the doll and said something into its microphone ear. "Suzy wants to say something to you."

Tricia smiled, trying not to appear impatient. Penny pressed the Play button in the doll's ring finger. "We love you, Tricia. You're the best sister in the world."

"I love you guys, too."

She put down the bag and gave Penny a hug.

For a moment, the sinking feeling that she might never see her little sister, or her parents again, devastated her. Her eyes brimmed with tears.

"What's a matter?" Penny asked.

She worked up a smile. "Nothing, you little turdpile. I've just got something in my eyes."

"Me, too," Penny replied, rubbing her eyes.

"You better get to bed," she said. "If Mom sees you awake, you won't see Morris the Moose for a month."

Her eyes got big, and she started to run back to her room before I stopped her.

"Penny..."

"What? I gotta go. I can't miss Morris."

"I love you, Penny."

She smiled. "I love you, too, Trisha Wisha."

Tricia kissed her cheek and let her scamper back to her room. She picked up her bags and hustled downstairs into the foyer. Her mother's purse was hanging on the hat rack where she kept it. She opened it and removed her credit card, her bank card, and the keys to her car. She wrote her parents a note telling them that she was all right and just needed some time alone to get her head together. She hoped they understood and would not call the police, knowing as she wrote the request, that it would be the first thing that they would do.

TWENTY-SEVEN

It was almost eleven when Tricia decided to drive past the Cornucopia on the off chance that Horf was still stocking the shelves for tomorrow. Two weeks ago, his boss had promoted him from bag boy to stock boy, moving his shift from afternoon to after hours. When she saw his car parked in the lot, she whooped with joy. She parked and ran to the window of the store. Horf was putting on his jacket getting ready to leave for home. She banged on the glass. He turned and saw her. A look of shock appeared on his face. He ran over to the door to let her into the store.

"Tricia, what the hell! Your mother came by the store earlier and asked her if you had come by. What's going on?" he asked, locking the door. "Why didn't you call me?"

"I'm in bad trouble. I know what's happening to me."

They walked to the aisle where Horf had been working and sat on a stack of boxes.

"So, clue me in," he said.

She jolted, realizing where she was sitting.

"What's wrong?" Horf asked.

Tricia sat smack dab in the middle of thousands of food items, an absolute smorgasbord of nightmares.

"We have to get out of here," she blurted. At the end of the canned soup aisle, the Oni emerged and glided toward her.

Tricia leapt to her feet.

Horf grabbed her arm. "Tricia, tell me what's going on."

"Let me go," she shouted. She yanked her arm from his grasp and pushed him into a stack of boxes. "I have to get out of here!"

The demon picked up speed. Tricia tore past a display of mineral water, knocking over several bottles.

Horf scrambled to his feet. "Tricia, stop, I want to help."

"No!" She screamed and ran for the exit. If the demon entered her inside the grocery store, she didn't know if she could stand the mental strain of so many horrendous visions barraging her at once. She slammed into the locked door. Hard. Her teeth clacked together. She staggered and turned to see the demon approaching.

"Let me out!" Tricia shouted, pounding on the glass.

Fingers appeared with a shiny metal key clasped in them. The key entered the lock, and the fingers turned it. When she heard the click, she pushed through the door and ran to her mom's car.

Horf grabbed her. "Tricia, snap out of it. You're okay. Now, tell me what's going on."

The demon lingered inside the store, watching, waiting.

She nodded wearily and explained the day's events. "I have to figure this out. I can't cause someone else to suffer like I am. I can't do it."

"But you can't starve to death, either. You need to get to a doctor, so they can give you an IV and force feed you."

"And I'll see snakes sucking on my arms or worms squirming under my skin, then I'll be the one flying out a three-story window to end my nightmare."

"The doctors can give you something to put you out. Then they can give you the fluids. How could the demon control an unconscious mind?"

"Then what? I spend the rest of my life as a drugged-out vegetable who couldn't bear to look at herself because she might turn into a steaming pile of rot?"

"At least you haven't lost your sense of humor."

She grabbed her hair in frustration. "Why was making the stupid dance team so important that I ruined my life?"

He held her firmly by her shoulders and looked her in the eye. "It's done. We have to find a way out of it."

"Tomoko says she tried everything. Nothing worked."

"So, find somebody to take your place. I know. Go to a nursing home and find a ninety-year-old on death's door and have her read the curse…"

She interrupted him. "Are you hearing yourself? You want me to make someone's last days on Earth as terrifying as possible. I won't do it. There's got to be another way to stop this thing."

Horf grabbed her suitcase out of the back seat of the Optima and moved it to the trunk of his car. He opened the door for her. "You wait here while I lock up. Then I'll take you wherever you want to go. I don't want you driving if that thing controls what you see. I'll call your mom and tell her where I parked her car later."

"And then she'll ask you where you took me. I had better park it at my house, and we leave from there. There's a chance my parents might hear us pull up, but we have to take it."

He nodded. Tricia got into her mom's car and waited for him to lock up and return to his vehicle. The Oni followed him out of the store, shimmered and dissipated into the night.

They drove their respective cars to Tricia's house. She parked the Optima without a hitch, hustled to his Sentra, got in and lightly closed the door.

"Where do you want to go?" Horf asked, letting the car idle away from the house before giving it gas.

"I need to find a cash machine and then a cheap hotel."

"Are you sure we're doing the right thing?"

"No, but I can't stay at my house. Mom and Dad think I have anorexia, and their good intentions of trying to get me to eat are going to drive me crazy … for real."

Deadly Diet

After Tricia withdrew the three-hundred-dollar limit from her mom's ATM account, she told Horf to take her to any motel outside of town, just as long as it was cheap. He drove her to the Bitterbrook Inn. It was a one-story job, unassuming and rundown, like the ones run by homicidal maniacs in horror movies. Perfect.

"Park at the entrance and stay in the car while I get the room," she said. "They might not let me book one if I have a boy with me."

"You see a boy give him a popsicle. I'm almost eighteen."

"Are you really playing the manhood card?"

"Sorry, my macho got away from me."

She smiled and kissed him. "Be right back."

She rapped on the door and looked inside the lobby. A sour-faced old man, rubbing his back, shuffled into the room, and blinked at her. He wore a grubby cotton robe on his thin frame. His bony white legs protruded from the tattered hem of the robe.

"Closed," he shouted.

"Please, I need a room."

"Closed, I said."

She took out the money and showed it to him. He stared at it for a moment with his tongue tucked in the corner of his mouth. He rubbed the salt-and-pepper stubble on his chin before going to the door and opening it.

"How old are you, girl?"

"Eighteen. Why?"

"Hmm, don't matter much, I guess." He shrugged. "Forty bucks for the night."

"How much for a week?"

"Week's two hundred twenty. Two fifty if you're a runaway." He laughed, a grotesque raspy chuckle. "My zippa-the-lip fee."

"Well, I'm not a runaway."

"Two fifty anyway, just in case."

"I'll pay you half now and half at the end of the week."

The old man yawned and shook his head. "All now."

All she had was three hundred dollars. Paying for the room would leave her with fifty dollars for the rest of the week.

"I need to get back to bed. You in or out?"

She paid him the money and returned to the car. They drove around and parked in front of room seven, lucky seven she hoped. While Tricia unlocked the hotel room door, Horf got her bag out of the trunk and carried it into the room. He slung it onto the bed.

"When I get home, I'll pack my bag and come back to stay with you."

"No. The demon might make me see you as a threat and who knows what I might do. I can't risk hurting you. Please stay away. This is something I have to do alone. I'll call you to let you know how I'm doing."

"But…"

"Please. You don't know how it can mess up my mind."

He stared at her, deciding if he wanted to put up a fight. "We'll play it your way. Just promise me if you need me for anything, and I mean anything, you'll call no matter what time it is."

"I will. I promise. And I promise something else. I'm either gonna beat the demon, or they're going to have to bury me."

TWENTY-EIGHT

The morning after Tricia left her house, Horf called her and told her that her parents had come to see him at the store, asking him where she was. He convinced them that he knew nothing about her whereabouts, even volunteering to help look for her. They thanked him but said it was a matter for the police now. Mom and Dad had researched "missing persons" online and discovered that going to the authorities as early as possible was the most effective course of action. There was no such thing as a waiting period like you see in the movies. Horf told her to keep her eyes open and be ready to bolt as the cops were sure to canvass motels and hotels around town.

The second day of her confinement proved him right. Tricia had stepped outside for a breath of fresh air and had seen a sheriff's car pull under the drive-through overhang and park. She ducked back into her room and peered from a sliver of window behind the curtain. A skinny deputy swaggered inside the lobby and stayed for a few minutes before returning to his car, followed by the owner who was shaking his head and patting the cop on his shoulder. As the cruiser drove off, the sour

165

old man, whose name was Trimble, spotted her peeking out the window. He gave her a sly thumbs-up before hobbling back to the lobby. He had been telling the truth about his zippa-da-lip fee.

It was now her fifth day at the Bitterbrook Inn. Five days of hunger, desperation, misery, boredom, and exhaustion with no plan in mind for defeating the demon. Out of frustration and with significant effort, Tricia slung the phonebook across the room, hitting the television that she couldn't watch because food was everywhere and everywhere lay madness. "I won't do it," she said to the demon watching her from the corner of the room. "I won't go there. You hear me?"

She got up and went to the bathroom to get a drink of water from the sink. She looked in the mirror and saw a living skeleton standing there. Her ribs protruded through her skin. Her arms were painfully thin. She knew that she was starving to death and there wasn't a thing she could do about it.

Oh, yes, there was. There was one thing she could do.

She stepped out of the bathroom and saw the phone book sitting on the floor. It was open to the Yellow Pages where she would find weight-loss centers sought by anxious overweight people to fulfil their dreams. All she had to do was find some overweight girl desperate enough to take ginseng pills and invite a demon into her life.

Katsu Hime giggled.

"Get out of here, you bitch!" Tricia screamed. She picked up the phone and hurled it at her.

The demon shattered into blue bits of light and then slowly reintegrated into her ghostly form.

A banging on the door startled her.

"Hey, what the hell are you doing in there?" It was Trimble.

"Leave me alone!" She shouted. "Everything's fine."

"I was cleaning the room next door and heard banging."

"I'm okay."

"I don't care if you're okay. I want to see what you're doing to my room."

A horrible thought struck her. *What if he is eating something?*

"Go away!" She shouted.

"I have the key. You either let me in, or I'll come in myself."

Deadly Diet

"Are you eating?"

"What?"

"Are you eating anything?"

"Jesus, what kinda question is that? No, I ain't eating."

She opened the door just as the Oni flew down from its perch and settled inside her.

"Now, what's all the noise about?" Trumble said.

He pushed her aside and entered the room. Before she could answer, she saw a delivery van outside. It was delivering snacks to the vending machines.

The owner put his hands on his hips. "This room is a mess, and it looks like you broke the phone. You're gonna have to pay for that." A huge bag of potato chips painted on the side of the van thrummed, the sides of the bag rippled and expanded.

"Oh, please, no."

"Oh please, yes. You breaka, you buy."

The bloated potato chip bag burst, and a horde of black flies poured from it.

Trimble stood in front of her. "Do you hear me, young lady?"

The boiling mass of flies buzzed toward her. She shoved the owner outside and slammed the door.

"Hey, what the hell? Let me in there, right now!" he yelled.

She backed away from the door.

A key rattled in the doorknob, the lock popped, and the door opened. "I want to know what's going on in here," he shouted.

The flies flooded through the door, enveloping the manager in a teeming black cloud. Tricia screamed and a few of the insects flew into her mouth. She gagged and staggered backward.

"You're bug-assed crazy. I knew it. Young girl like you on drugs," the owner said, his stubble now a full black beard of insects. "Should have told the cops you were here. Saved my phone."

She spat drowned flies from her mouth and scooped handfuls from her face, crushing them.

"I want you out of here today!" Trimble said.

The flies swarmed all over her. She swatted them with both hands.

"I'm calling the damn cops," the owner said.

As she batted the swarming flies, he ran out of the room.

She closed her eyes and concentrated on anything but food. She filled her mind with visions of the moon's surface. Vast, barren, desolate. Nothing there but rocks and dust.

Slowly the chill of the Oni left her. She opened her eyes. The flies had vanished.

She shoved her things into her suitcase, the phone book included, put on her coat, and ran out of the room. She didn't want to be there when the police came. They would take her home and her parents would take her back to the clinic where they would force feed her into madness.

When she got outside, she saw Trimble picking up trash that had blown onto his driveway. He saw her and waved.

Her face buzzed. What was going on? Why wasn't he getting the police?

Katsu Hime emerged from behind the owner, a devilish black grin on her face.

The line between reality and illusion was blurring more with each passing ounce of fat.

Tricia returned to her room, threw herself onto the bed and stifled a scream with her pillow. A sudden urge to give up overwhelmed her. She had been in the hotel room for five long, tedious, horrible days with nothing to do but think of some way out of this dilemma, and she'd come up with nothing.

Her eyes settled on the phone book sitting next to her on the bedstand. She picked it up and opened it to the section on weight-loss centers. She located what looked to be the most prosperous clinic, wrote down the address on a slip of stationery, and then called for a taxi.

The last thing she did was to make sure she had the parchment in her pocket.

TWENTY-NINE

Tricia stood outside the Fresh Start Weight Loss Center in downtown Portland and watched any number of overweight girls enter. All she had to do was work up the nerve to approach one of them and start a conversation about the difficulties of losing weight. Get the girl to open up about her struggles. Win her trust by telling her how she used to wrestle with the same problems until she was ready to give up on her dream of being thin. That was when she discovered a miraculous way to lose as many pounds as she wanted. Then Tricia would play the sly fox, get the girl to beg her for the secret and then, when she had her victim champing at the bit, spring the story of the pills on her and give her the parchment to read.

A likely candidate emerged from her car. She was about her age and wore a baggy sweatsuit that did little to hide her bulky frame. She waddled toward the front door of the clinic. Tricia started toward her when an instructor in gym clothes bounded out of the clinic and greeted the girl. "Judy, how are you doing?"

"Good. I lost two more pounds this week."

"Great. That's excellent."

The girl smiled. "I really think I'm going to lose the weight this time."

The expression of desperate hopefulness on the girl's face shattered Tricia's resolve. She couldn't go through with it. She couldn't inflict the curse on someone else and make them suffer as she had suffered. This girl had a family like she did. Parents that loved and cared for her. She might have a cute little sister like Penny and a dopey doll with a tape recorder in it that allowed her to talk to you if…

Tricia stopped in mid-thought, thunderstruck by a bolt of revelation.

"Yes! Oh, God, yes, that's it!" She cried, causing the instructor and the girl to look her way. "Does one of you have a phone I could borrow? Mine's out of battery."

"Sure," the girl said. She pulled her phone out of her pocket.

Tricia ran to call Horf to ask him to take her home, but in her exhausted state, she didn't see the parking block and tripped over it. The asphalt rose up and slammed her chin. Her teeth crashed together, detonating sparks in her head. The blacktop opened and swallowed her. When the darkness spat her out into the light, she was lying on a couch in front of the health food bar of the weight-loss clinic.

"She's coming around," a pretty blond woman in a business suit said. Her badge identified her as the assistant director. The banana pin next to her badge was pulsating. It burst open and a jet of blood hit Tricia in the face.

She tried to sit up, but the woman gently pushed her back onto the couch. She smiled and several of her teeth fell out onto Tricia's chest.

She could feel the presence of the Oni inside her, colder and more powerful. She knew if she wanted to stop her demon, she would have to do it that day. If Katsu Hime got any stronger, Tricia didn't think she'd have the strength to get rid of her.

"You need to take it easy," the woman said. "We have a doctor on staff who will be here in a second. You took a nasty fall out there."

Judy, her would-be victim of the Oni, stood over her. She was sipping a fruit shake that was made from the viscera of a diseased animal.

Deadly Diet

"She just started running and hit the curb," the girl said, then slurped up a long intestine.

Tricia rolled her head to one side and saw thick orange worms the size of carrots crawling toward her from the direction of the snack bar. The worms had small white teeth, all the same size and serrated like those of a shark. She closed her eyes to ward off the visions and that's when things took a decidedly darker turn. One of the carrot-worms bit her face and she felt the sharp pain of the serrated teeth shredding the flesh on her cheek. She opened her eyes and saw another worm squirming right in front of her face. It opened its jaws and sank its jagged teeth into the pupil of her eye. It felt like a pencil had stabbed her. She shrieked and pressed her palm against her closed eyelid, rolling in agony on the couch.

"Call an ambulance. She's in pretty severe pain."

More of the orange worms crawled onto the couch and attacked her, biting her skin and scalp, tearing little chunks of flesh. She couldn't stand it anymore. She fought her way to her feet.

"Miss, please, we're trying to help."

The girl behind the counter dialed her phone. The basket of rotten fruit on the snack bar started to move. The putrid apples and pears in the basket split open. Gelatinous, skinless bats emerged from the spoiled fruit and stretched their membranous wings.

"I have to get home," Tricia shouted and took off running.

But how do I get out of here?

Having been unconscious when they carried her inside, she didn't know her way out of the building.

The jellied bats took flight and pursued her. She ran toward a door and entered a storeroom where they kept the boxes of low-fat food. A multitude of creatures—fanged chicken legs, bleeding anemones of squirming pasta, vomiting cheese—lunged for her. She turned to run, and the squishy bats attacked her face, digging their claws into her cheeks. As she ran, she crushed and slung them into the walls of the corridor.

"There she is," someone said.

"Miss, please, you may have a concussion."

The doctor's face began to peel away, revealing the oozing fat, muscle, and bone underneath. Above his head, Tricia saw the red lettered sign EXIT.

She slowed and then, with a final burst of energy, sprinted past the doctor and blasted through the door.

She staggered outside into the back parking lot of the center. Across the street was a fast-food restaurant, but to her it was a huge, misshapen thing, a giant mass of greasy tentacles and pulsating flesh. It was chewing up the people who entered it, spitting out bloody carcasses from the drive-through windows. She turned away and ran to the other side of the building. She stopped and focused all her willpower to drive Katsu Hime out of her mind. The telltale chill left her.

She walked quickly across the street to a strip-mall church and managed to borrow a cell phone from the pastor's wife. She recalled Horf's number which she had memorized since her failure to remember it what seemed years ago. After three shaky tries, she managed to stab the right numbers on the keypad.

"Horf! Oh, thank God. I have a way to stop this thing I think, but I have to get to my house."

"Are you at the hotel?"

"No. I took a cab to Fresh Start Weight Loss Center on Main, but I'm across the street at The Church of Agape."

"Did you...?"

"No, I didn't transfer the curse."

"Good. I'll be there in five minutes," Horf said. He hung up.

She had to listen to the pastor's wife preach about asking Jesus for help with her drug problem until Horf came to get her. She jumped into his car just as an ambulance and a police car showed up at the clinic.

"Are they here for you?" Horf asked.

"The people at Fresh Start called them. They think I hurt my head."

"Looks like you hurt your chin." He touched it tenderly. "Are you okay?"

"I'm fine."

"Duck down," Horf said.

Deadly Diet

He drove past the emergency vehicles and the concerned throng of people. When they got onto the main road, he said, "Okay, the coast is clear."

Driving down the streets of town gave her time to think about the guy sitting next to her and what a tool she had been to not see how fantastic he was. "Horf, I want you to know something."

"What's that?"

"If we ever get out of this shitstorm, I would be honored if you'd take me out on a real date to kickstart our relationship."

"Gee, a relationship with kissing and everything," Horf deadpanned.

She smiled. "Yeah, with kissing and everything. Like this."

She pulled him toward her and kissed him on the lips.

"We're gonna crash if you do that again." Horf grinned, then added, "So watch out for the airbag."

She laughed. It felt good.

"So, my future real date, tell me this plan of yours."

THIRTY

When they got to Tricia's house, it was a little past four o'clock. Her mom must have retrieved her car and parked it in the driveway. Her presence was going to make it a bit stickier to accomplish Tricia's plan, but if Mom was home that meant Penny was home and that was crucial to her plan. She and Horf entered the house.

"Mom?" Tricia called.

There was no answer.

"Mom? Penny?"

No one was there.

"I don't get it. The car's parked out front. Now what are we going to do?"

"Get the fire roaring in the fireplace," Horf said looking out the window onto the backyard. "Your mom and Penny are heading this way."

"Has she got it?"

"I can't tell. Your mom's in the way."

"Toss another log on the fire and then check upstairs in her room."

174

Deadly Diet

He gave her a thumbs up. She did the same but doubts about her plan's effectiveness crept into her head. She knew that opening the refrigerator door was going to be one of the hardest things she'd ever have to do, but she needed to buy time for Horf to find the doll.

As she stepped into the kitchen, she sensed a presence standing behind her. She didn't have to look to know what was there. She ignored the demonic princess and opened the refrigerator just as Horf entered the kitchen. "She's not in her room!"

"No," Tricia whispered. Katsu Hime's possession iced her body.

An overwhelming stench hit her in the face. The inside of the fridge looked like a torn and rotting carcass of some mutated beast. Red and purple veiny things squirmed and bubbled. Black and blue masses of undetermined origin pulsated and oozed green glop.

Just then, the kitchen door opened, and Mom and Penny stepped inside from the back yard.

"Tricia! You're home!" Mom shouted. She ran over and gave her a hug. Tricia grimaced in pain. "My poor baby. You're nothing but skin and bones! We have to get you to the hospital right away."

"Tricia's here, Tricia's here," Penny cried. "Look, Suzy. Tricia's back."

Several slick black eggplant crows emerged from the vegetable bin. They flapped toward her and began stabbing her with their sharp beaks. She punched at them, hitting her mother with closed fists. Mom staggered and tried to grab her flailing arms. "Tricia, calm down. Horf, help me."

Horf ignored her. He ripped the Suzy Chatterbox doll from Penny's hands and ran out of the kitchen.

"Mommy, he took my doll," Penny cried. "Horf kidnapted Suzy."

The crows battered her with their beaks. The pain was staggering. Tricia knew that the Oni had almost complete possession of her.

A maddening mass of creatures toppled out of the refrigerator onto the floor and started squirming toward her. She screamed and kicked at them.

"What's going on here?" Mom shouted. "Tricia, stop it!"

"I want my dolly!" Penny sobbed.

An inside-out chicken with razor-sharp claws cackled and shredded her legs. Tricia kicked away at it, slamming her foot into her mother's shin. She cried out in pain and grabbed her, but she didn't see her mother; she saw a huge scab-covered corpse that smelled of formaldehyde and fried chicken. She pushed the Kentucky-fried cadaver away from her. Everything spun out of control. Mom's corrupted corpse, the crows, the chicken, all the unrecognizable horrors that bubbled from the refrigerator whirled in a tight circle in front of her.

The chill of the Oni left her.

"Dear Lord," Mom cried, when she saw Katsu Hime emerge from her body and glide out of the kitchen.

Penny screamed. "They're real! Ghosts are real!"

Tricia staggered after the demon. She knew where she was going.

Horf had recited the words on the parchment.

He stood in the middle of the living room, his hands behind his back as though he was waiting for the Captain of the Guard to hand him a cigarette and a blindfold for his execution by firing squad. The demonic spirit sped toward him, a grin of satisfaction on her face.

Suddenly, Horf took the doll from behind his back and squeezed her hand.

Suzy Chatterbox recited the *daburu kurosu*.

The Oni changed course and slammed into the doll. Tricia tried to imagine Katsu Hime's confusion when she realized there was no brain to control. In those seconds of puzzlement, Trish and Horf had their window of opportunity.

"Horf, the fireplace!" She shouted.

He spun on his heel and pitched the doll into the roaring fire.

"Suzy!" Penny cried. She ran to rescue her friend.

Mom grabbed her daughter and held her tightly to keep her from looking at what was happening in the fireplace. "No, let it burn."

Katsu Hime shrieked and clawed trying to escape from the inanimate doll. The flames melted away the plastic and revealed a thing that was like something from another planet: sparkling lights, black holes that could have been eyes, and weird appendages that looked like feet and hand combinations. This thing burst open and oozed a grayish-red matter that sizzled when it hit the burning logs. The inner core of the thing exploded sending flames whooshing up into the chimney. The fire died down and all traces of Takeda Katsu Hime were gone.

"What in the world was that thing?" Mom gasped, still holding Penny tightly against her hip.

"I'll tell you all about it," Tricia said. "But first I have to thank someone." She ran to Horf, threw her arms around his neck, and gave him a thanks-for-saving-my-life kiss.

When they came up for air, he hugged her and said, "You're welcome."

"Can I ask you one thing though?"

"What's that?"

"If we're gonna start dating, do you mind if I call you Harv? I don't want to have to explain to people why I'm dating a guy named Horf."

He looked at her and shook his head. "I thought you learned your lesson about caring what other people think."

Tricia smiled. "You're right. You're exactly right. When I get my phone back, I'm going to call Megan and Mandy and tell them I'm dating a guy named Horf."

"Now, will you please tell me what is going on?" Mom pleaded.

"Sure, Mom," Tricia said, "but if you don't mind, I'd like to tell you over a cup of soup and a little piece of toast." She smiled broadly. "I'm starving."

ABOUT THE AUTHOR

Vince Courtney was born with pencil and paper in hand which made for a very uncomfortable delivery for his mother. He is the author of eighteen books.

Bibliography

<u>**Adult horror and thriller**</u>
Goblins
Harvest of Blood
Let's Pretend You're Dead
Vampire Beat
Wake Up Screaming

<u>**YA horror**</u>
Deadly Diet
Die Laughing
The Room

Children's horror
A Tale from Camp Crypt
A Tale from the Crypt Carnival
A Tale from the Crypt Class Trip

Children's humor
Laugh Attack
Saint Nicked
Virtual Fred
Virtual Fred and the Big Dip

TV adaptation
Flesh and Bone
Heart and Soul
Street Sharks

Curious about other Crossroad Press books? Stop by our website:
http://crossroadpress.com
We offer quality writing
in digital, audio, and print formats.

Subscribe to our newsletter on the website homepage and receive a
free eBook.

Made in the USA
Middletown, DE
19 March 2024

51234008R00111